THE LION HEART

ROGUE ACADEMY, BOOK TWO

CARRIE AARONS

Copyright © 2019 by Carrie Aarons

All rights reserved.

No part of this book may be reproduced in any form or by any electronic or mechanical means, including information storage and retrieval systems, without written permission from the author, except for the use of brief quotations in a book review.

This is a work of fiction. Names, characters, businesses, places, events and incidents are either the products of the author's imagination or used in a fictitious manner. Any resemblance to actual persons, living or dead, or actual events is purely coincidental.

Editing done by Proofing Style.

Cover designed by Okay Creations.

Do you want your **FREE** Carrie Aarons eBook?

All you have to do is **sign up for my newsletter**, and you'll immediately receive your free book!

To the warriors who have survived trauma and come out infinitely stronger on the other side.

PROLOGUE
POPPY

One Year Ago

Darkness shrouds the group of us, fresh off a magazine shoot in our teased hair and over-dramatic makeup.

I can smell the perfume and various products wafting off the girls as they walk in front of me, following the waitress to our VIP booth in this cliché celebrity club that I've come to loathe. I'm not even sure why I came in the first place, probably because my fear of missing out got the best of me.

I never could fall to one side or the other of the fence; I either craved the limelight and sought out fame, or wanted to cower from it, locked away from the lenses forever.

"Hey, you're the new Riare campaign model," a deep, polished accent shouts in my direction over the pulsing music.

Biting back an eye roll, I let my neck lazily, but gracefully, shift to one side. It's never a question of when I'll be recognized, but of which sloshed bar scum will try to throw cheesy pickup lines at me first.

Except, when my eyes finally connect with said scum, he is

not the usual type. I have to physically school my features into distaste and nonchalance while assessing the man.

And he is a man, in all sense of the word. His long limbs spill over the couch in an almost vulgar position, his thick thighs spread and straining against the dark jeans he's wearing. It's as if he's inviting me to sit on his lap and feel just what's between those muscled legs. My eyes travel to his hands, large and capable, planted squarely on his knees. His frame commands attention, from the way his arms and torso fill out the royal blue collared shirt to the way he's sexily slouched against the plush velvet of the booth.

When my gaze reaches his face, I find his electric-green eyes, their color almost unattainably clover-like, winking with suggestion. His olive skin creases at his cheeks, where his mouth and chiseled jawbone are turned up in a wicked smirk. The sandy blond crop of hair is smoothed back with gel, giving him that debonair look all the athletes seem to go for these days.

The attire he dons is one of affluence, casual jeans and a button-up that probably retails for thousands, and I can tell from his accent that he grew up with a silver spoon in his mouth. Yes, I know who he is. This is Kingston Phillips, one of those footie legacy children who believes he owns London and all the women in it.

What makes him dangerous, though, is the kind of charm that comes with that upbringing and attitude. If you believe you're untouchable, you take risks. Risks that the public can see, and ones you're not afraid of answering for. Sure, I know very little about Kingston Phillips, but I encounter men like him every day. It's the ones who operate in the light, not the shadows, that you should be afraid of.

I've clocked this guy in three seconds flat, he has nothing to hide and is probably one of those cocky blokes who is embarrassed by very little, if nothing at all.

But the fact that he thinks he has me figured out? Some floozy model who'll fall all over herself for a chance to kneel in front of him? Christ, there is nothing I hate more than when people think they know me.

"And you're that cheeky football player who thinks he can bed anyone who bats an eyelash at him," I quip back, unamused.

Joining the other models—they're not my friends, we're merely out together to be seen as such—at our table, I give him my back and open a menu.

"Oh, I like her." The lone female with them giggles drunkenly.

I cast a quick glance at her. She's beautiful in an unconventional way, and I envy her. When someone looks at her, they're not just imagining which campaign or product she can sell. Jude Davies, anyone would know who the next great athlete of our time is, laughs and pulls her closer to him. She nuzzles sweetly in the crook of his arm, and I have to swallow the jealousy bubbling up in my throat.

Pasting on a smile, I get up, because while I may be direct, I'm not rude. "Poppy Raymond, nice to meet you."

"You look like an Amazon." She blinks, shaking my extended hand.

I think she's too pissed to remember to tell me her name, but that's all right.

"You're beautiful, in a way only someone like you could be. Elegant, angelic, with the sex appeal of a loaded pistol but the grace to disguise it. When people see a woman like me, they automatically think slag or model; my looks are far too obvious." I tell her the truth.

"Now I get it!" Kingston cries from where he sits on the other side of Jude. "You're a lesbian."

Now, I really want to slap this wanker. He looks so pleased

with himself for finding the obvious reason I'm not interested in him, and it only makes me want to wind up and kick him right in the bollocks.

My lip curls up, and I know that cold gleam in my eye is boring holes into him. "I'm not a lesbian. I just know how to admire beauty, in a way that doesn't scream at everyone that I'm a bloody git. However, if I were I would have ten times the game you do when trying to pick someone up."

The arsehole looks like I've sucker punched him in the gut. His jaw hangs wide open, and the expression of sheer shock tells me he doesn't get turned down. *Ever.*

"Oh my lord, I think he's met his match." Their fourth tablemate chuckles as he tips his beer back.

"Why don't you come sit down on my lap and find out just how much game I have?" Kingston waggles his eyebrows at me, undeterred from my obvious distaste.

This guy is bloody incorrigible. And, he has no idea what lies just under the surface of my pretty little facade. If he did, he wouldn't come within fifty feet. A guy like this would never deal with the festering wounds I've hidden under the makeup and expensive clothing.

"Make it to the first squad, come play in London among the ranks of the big boys, and maybe I'll give your theory a test." I smirk, practiced in the art of masking my true feelings.

I flounce back to my booth, pretending to be completely ignorant of the fact that anyone exists beyond the group of girls I'm dining with.

But in the pit of my stomach, it's all still there. The fear, the annoyance, the inability to trust. And the sorrow at not being able to let anyone close enough to test the theory that there are still, in fact, good men among thieves.

1

KINGSTON

Leggy blond.
 Leggy brunette.
 Leggy blond.
Oh, switching it up with a leggy redhead.

Yes, I could sit here all night and watch these gorgeous models strut their perfectly molded asses down the runway. In lingerie, no less. Expertly tailored scraps of lace in all the colors of the rainbow. One would think that undressing these goddesses down to their knickers would leave nothing to the imagination, but if anything, the barely-there undergarments did just that.

Each time one of the Boudoir Lingerie Bombshell's saunters past my front-row seat, my heart beats a little faster. Every time I tilt my head back, trying to admire the view from below the stage that's been lifted five feet from the floor, the blood in my veins heats another degree. And my cock? The bloody bastard's been hard as a steel pipe since the electric techno music introduced the first sex kitten in her virginal white getup.

"I mean, how many pairs of underwear can a woman have?" Jude rolls his eyes next to me, his head buried in his phone.

"Are you bloody insane?" I slap at his hands, making him almost drop his phone.

My best mate sighs annoyedly. "I was supposed to meet Aria half an hour ago. We've watched the same fifteen birds traipse out here in different shades of satin for almost two hours. They all look the same. When does this thing end?"

Only a man that was thoroughly whipped could turn up his nose at an endless stream of ridiculously hot models. How could Jude say that they all looked the same? Was that what happened when you fell in love? You became blind to all women but one? Count me out ... God, the thought made me want to lose my dinner.

To me, each woman looked like a new conquest I could explore in bed. To me, they all looked like a challenge.

"You're being rude. The photographers are going to catch pictures of you texting through this thing. Be a good boy, put away your phone, and observe the buffet of tits in front of you," I scold him as my eyes turn to said-buffet, watching as plentiful sets of boobs jiggle down the catwalk.

We were both asked to attend the annual Boudoir Lingerie Fashion Show as honored guests. The warehouse is lit in bubbly pink spotlights and fluorescent white shades. The chairs lining the stage and extending up toward the rafters house all kinds of celebrities, from musicians to actors to athletes. As two of the top footie players for Rogue Football Club, the best squad in all of England, it was our duty to show up for publicity events like this. It got our names in the papers, which generated press for the club and interest in us, which translated to ticket sales. And ticket sales means money for the club which means better coaches and facilities, or key players brought in on trades. I might act like a git most of the time, but I know how this world works. I've been raised in it, I know all about optics and strategy.

Playing football is not my only job, and it was drilled into me from a young age to remember that.

Plus, the perks of sitting front row, and then attending the VIP after-party, to watch the most attractive women in the world walk around nearly naked—yeah, I wasn't passing those up.

"I don't even know why I'm here. Couldn't they have just sent you? You'll shag enough of these models for us both." He tucks his phone into his pockets and folds his hands in his lap, keeping his gaze dutifully straight ahead.

He's the company man, the one who would live or die for the club even if they asked for something he didn't really want to do. After a few years of recklessness, Jude Davies has straightened up in the past twelve months and become the next football legend we all knew he'd be. Scoring goals like a madman, showing up to all the press events his agent books him for, teaching football camps to little kids, and just generally becoming the face of the sport in England. Never mind, that he's just twenty-one ... if you know what's good for you, you know Jude Davies is the be all, end all when it comes to British football these days.

Me? Well, I've always been the guy with too much talent, and not enough work ethic. At least that's what every trainer I've ever encountered has told me. I can rely on the God-given, or genetic, skills that I've been blessed with to get me through each match, but I never put forth more effort than that. It seems daft; why exert more energy when you're already pretty good? Plus, I've never taken myself too seriously. It's not like I'm a forward, it's not like I have to score goals to keep my job.

I play left back. My tasks are to cock up the other team's offense, talk shite, be bloody fast, tackle players without the referee catching me, and having dead aim for my forwards so they can sprint up the field with my passes. By nature, my position is one of sneakiness, of annoyance, and it fits my personality.

Kingston Phillips, the jester. The jokester. The pot-stirrer. That's me, and I play it well. It's the role I was given, much to my parent's disappointment and I've put my all into adopting the persona.

"That's right, I will." Rubbing my hands together, I give him a devious smile.

Nothing more in this world I like than putting my hands and mouth on a beautiful female, preferably more than one at a time. Oh, the games I can play then.

"Well, maybe not her." Jude smirks in that prick way of his, like he knows something I don't.

Glancing toward the alcove at the back of the runway, my eyes home in on who he's talking about.

Shite, I'd almost forgotten she wore the coveted Bombshell title. It took most models years to work their way into the brand. If you were named a Boudoir Bombshell, it basically defined you as one of the most desired women in the world.

But she'd been given the title at eighteen, as soon as it was legally acceptable to bestow it upon her.

Poppy Raymond. The one woman in the world who hates my guts.

Actually, that's not exactly true. I'm sure there are *loads* of chicks out there who want to slap me in the face or slash my tires. But that's after I sleep with them and then don't call them back or they catch me being photographed with another woman.

But Poppy Raymond ... she's the only one who wants nothing to do with me *before* we've shed each other's clothes. I bet if I could flash her a glimpse of what's going on below my waist, she wouldn't be so ice cold.

Or, maybe, she'd just slash that appendage off. The thought makes me shiver.

Sitting here, in the front row of a fashion show where she is the star of the finale, is probably the closest I'll ever get to unwrapping what's underneath all of that stubborn, sassy facade.

As usual, she's the most stunning woman in the room. Not that I'd tell her that, or needed too. She already knows it, and of the few brief interactions we've had, nothing I'd done to woo her had worked.

Her feet—Christ, I'd never been so bloody interested in a woman's feet before hers—are strapped into impossibly high heels. The kind of heels that make your eyes focus instantly on the way her long, bronze legs carry her entire body. Lean and sculpted in a way that makes you imagine those legs wrapped around your own waist, your eyes can only do one thing next. Home in on the arse to make all other arses irrelevant. Round and perky and accented by the tiniest light blue scrap of lace I've ever seen.

That torso, the one that cinches and dips like a vintage soda bottle, leads up to tits that almost make you forget about the arse. Larger than a handful and perfectly trussed up in a bra I'd pay good money to have her wear forever. Long dark hair, the color of melted chocolate swirled with sticky caramel, falls in tendrils over her shoulders and spills down over the curves of her cleavage.

And that face, lord have mercy on men. The angelic face that has graced hundreds of magazines, billboards, and TV screens, with those sapphire blue eyes and the naughty little dimple in her right cheek ...

It's pointed right at me as she floats over the runway. A quick glance at the top of her waving locks and I spot the gleaming sapphire-jeweled crown they've placed upon it.

Yes, Poppy Raymond is the queen.

And with the way she's looking at me, you'd think it was off with my head.

2

POPPY

Bloody hell, I wish I could remove the cake that's seeping into my pores.

There is more makeup cemented onto my face than I've ever worn in my life. And I'm a professional model, so that's saying something.

Every year, I detest this show more and more, and I've only been walking in it for three years. First off, it's always a week after my birthday, when all I really want to be doing is sunning myself on some tropical island and not worrying about dehydrating my body to get the leanest look I can for the cameras.

What's more, I actually can't stand the Boudoir brand and what they stand for. Their lingerie is uncomfortable, unattainable, and just downright sleazy on most occasions. There is nothing high-fashion about it, which is why I originally got into this industry ... to visually represent my love for innovative clothing and material.

That's not what this brand, or its founder, is about, though. Cheap materials and lazy designs peddled for the masses at a ridiculously inflated cost. Models done up to the nth degree so that anyone trying to achieve the picturesque idea of sex

Boudoir is selling couldn't even come close. *I don't even look like this*, I think to myself as I turn my face side to side in the mirror before me.

But being a Boudoir Bombshell made your résumé shine. When I went on other casting calls or was approached by a design house to possibly walk for them during fashion week, having this show and its notoriety in my look book was priceless. It's why I keep coming back.

Thankfully, it's over now. I'll have to deal with the press dogging me about the flirty, jaw-dropping runway for weeks, but at least the worst of it is through.

Not that this will be the last of the jobs I don't want to work on. But because I was gifted with height, and a body that others envy, why not use them while they served me?

My mother was all about using what we had to serve ourselves. I'd tried to reiterate her own words back to her when I excitedly explained to my parents about the first makeup campaign I'd ever landed, but she told me I had used that motto to my own benefit. Modeling wasn't a sound choice, in either career or modesty. Maybe she meant our brains, or our ability to help those in the church; she was nothing if not devoutly religious.

Still, I went for it. At fourteen, I signed myself up for a local commercial casting call, and landed the gig. I'd fraudulently signed the release with my mother's name, appeared in the advertisement for a semi-popular fried chicken franchise in the part of England I grew up in, and the rest is history.

So, here I sit, as *the* Boudoir Bombshell. It's both the best, and worst, part of my life.

Backstage is swarming with people, from the other models to their friends, to reporters, to other celebrities trying to start the party early. Honestly, I think I see someone lighting up a joint in the corner and the champagne has already popped several times.

Don't they get bored of it all? I'm deathly bored.

Movement out of the corner of my eye, and a ripple through the crowd, has me sneaking a glance under my eyelashes.

Ah, the golden boys have arrived. Kingston Phillips commands the attention of everyone in the room, sucking it in and puffing out his chest like he's just stolen the helium from a balloon. Jude Davies looks more reserved beside him, but he still sparkles and shines just the same.

It's the newest member of the Rogue Football Club who has me almost doing a double take, though. Not that I'd admit it, or let anyone see me do so, but …

Bloody hell, the man is by far the most ridiculously goodlooking specimen I've ever seen. Tonight, he's decided on a charcoal gray suit with a black button-down underneath, and he looks like some younger, sexier version of Daniel Craig as James Bond, if that's even possible. He's way overdressed compared to the douchebag singers and billion-dollar techies in here, but of course, he pulls it off. Half the girls in this room are already drooling over him. His coloring, his bone structure, the sheer brawniness of him; it's a mix of Swedish and Italian heritage. And the combo? It's impossible not to acknowledge just how gorgeous the man is.

Even if Kingston Phillips is the crudest, slimiest bugger I've ever met.

"Look what the cat dragged in," I deadpan as soon as he spots me and begins his prowl over to me.

Better to have the first, and last, word when it comes to Kingston. Our few brief encounters have left me shaken, even if he's had no idea of my inner trembling. But, fake it enough and soon you'll start believing it yourself.

Our eyes connect, a clash of my clear blue and his emerald-hued greens, and a flutter works its way from my stomach to my throat. He drapes his arm over the back of my director style chair, the one I've had my arse planted in for hours while a team of five does my hair and makeup to the point where I'm almost unrecognizable.

"Well, love, I made it to the first squad. Now, how's about that shag?"

No preamble, no congratulations on the show, it's all about the pussy and the cock with this one. Isn't that the modus operandi for most men, if not all in this shade of limelight? It's why I avoid them, and especially why I avoid him. Because as much as I've tried to put him in the sleazy, dangerous column in my mind, he keeps popping into my dreams—ones I can't control and wake up in a cold sweat from.

Of course, he made it to the first squad of the Rogue Football Club only about two months after I'd ribbed him in that posh club where our booths had sat side by side. But there was still one thing I could tease him about.

Not bothering to actually face him, but rudely looking at him in the mirror while I fix my lipstick, I bite back, "Oh, did I say first squad? I'm sorry, I only go to bed with starters."

It's widely known that Kingston Phillips has ridden the bench for a good part of eight months and that he is a disgrace to his legendary mum and dad. I don't know the whole backstory, honestly, I have tried to avoid getting to know anything about the slick-tongued superstar, but his mum is some kind of Olympic football legend from Sweden, and his dad ... well, everyone knows who Edward Phillips is, even if you don't follow sports at all.

Edward Phillips is the Roman Stallion, the most handsome football legend to ever grace Italy's pitches. He was the heartthrob my own mum used to swoon over whenever he'd commentate games for Sky Sports.

The Lion Heart

It's always struck me as odd, that they have the last name Phillips. It's not very Italian, but apparently Edward's Welsh father fell in love with a Sicilian duchess or something ... there are always rumors of her abdication to be with him, but I've never studied them thoroughly. Though, it explains the dark, Italian features with the British surname.

And it's no damn wonder how Kingston was graced with his annoyingly good looks.

That face, the one that's almost pretty except too lean in the cheekbones and jaw to be considered boyishly handsome, wears a sour expression as it glances back at me in the mirror.

Then, it splits into a wide smile, revealing a set of teeth that had to have been bought. "You're a hell raiser, I just know it. It's what I like about you, Poppy."

"Good night, Kingston." I can't stand to be in this room one more minute, not when my skin feels like it's crawling, and the claustrophobia is kicking in.

Especially, since the last person I care to break down in front of is him. Just like all men, he's the type to capitalize on weakness. I just know it.

My legs carry me away from him, away from the mass of people that are about to turn the night into a powder keg, and out to the car that I specifically detailed, in my rider, to be waiting for me minutes after the show.

The streets of London are alive with the merriment of a Saturday night as the driver whips my private car through roundabouts and past double deckers. The cheers and hoorah's of locals outside pubs can be heard even through the tinted, bulletproof glass. Part of me is glad I have the barrier between us, it makes my heart rate decelerate from grand prix speed.

A total of twenty minutes door to door and the door of the car is being pulled open by the driver who bids me a good night and passes me to the doorman of my building. The inside of my new home beckons with its crystal chandeliers and spotless marble floors.

The lobby in Charlton House is almost empty when I enter it, save for the night receptionist and the lone doorman who both greet me amicably, but keep their distance. The building is an establishment for the elite, and the staff are trained to abide by the highest standards.

As I ride up in the elevator, and then walk to flat number 602, the breath I didn't realize I'd been holding whooshes out of my lungs.

This flat was my first monumental purchase in the six years I've been in the modeling business. Yes, I've made more than my weight in money, but I never thought about putting down roots because I'm typically on an airplane or a different city every other day. Who needs a pad when they're not even home half the year?

But then I'd returned to London for a month-long campaign with a popular chain makeup store, I was offered a three-lipstick deal named after me, and my agent set me up in model housing. I don't mean that the housing was model, that it was impeccable or some top-of-line penthouse. No, I mean that there were seven other models living in this brownstone in Chelsea and I had to listen to girls shagging and barfing up their food half the time.

That put me on the market for my own place right quick. I knew I wanted to be in the Belgravia neighborhood of London, and there was no better building here than Charlton House. Lucky me that one of the four flats on the top floor of the building was vacant, and I'd bought it without hesitation.

I moved my things in a week ago, and I know now that I've never made a better decision. There is still so much work I want done, and design options I have to nail down, but the space is purely, *safely*, mine.

My palm connects with the door as soon as I swing it closed

behind me, and as hard as I try, I still slam it shut. It's a habit, one that makes me feel marginally better as the night closes in around me. I twist the first deadbolt, and then the second and third, before letting out a measured breath.

And the tension slips out of me like air in a balloon as I feel fur rub against my shin. Josephine, my Scottish Fold cat, nuzzles her fuzzy white body against my leg and purrs. I like to think she's telling me she loves me whenever I walk in the door, but in all reality, she probably just wants her food dish refilled.

"Hi, Jojo." I bend down, picking her up and planting a kiss against her velvety head.

She purrs again, and a sense of deep loneliness goes through me. Is it sad that my cat is the only person in the world I feel understands me? Gosh, I sound like one of those nutters who hoards felines in their apartment until the health department evicts them.

It's true, though. Modeling, and the celebrity stratosphere in general, is so competitive, none of those people can actually be called your friends. Sure, we schmooze and rub elbows and play nice, but those bitches would cut you down or sell you out in a minute to land a job everyone was vying for. Although I'm not proud of it, I've done the same thing.

So, industry types are out. But so are friends from back home. Not that I had many solid ones, since I'd left Wrexham before secondary schools. Though if I did, many of them didn't know how to properly associate with me once I'd been in the spotlight. They'd either sold stories about me and my family to the tabloids or become wildly jealous. It was a double-edged sword, and not one I wanted to encounter, so I cut most ties.

That left my parents and my sister, the only sibling I have. Since my parents have never been keen on my modeling anyway, it's been difficult to confide in them about problems, or even triumphs. And my sister is too busy sitting on their pedestal, running the youth program at their church and becoming engaged to a nice local boy. Most parents would be incredibly proud of the career I've carved out for myself, of how much money I make or how I have supported myself from a very young age. My parents aren't most parents.

All in all, that left no one but me. And Josephine. I guess that is rather fine, then, since I can tell her my secrets and she has no voice to judge them, or spill them to anyone else.

Because the things I tell her are the scary kind that go bump in the night. The kind that ruin psyches and brand someone as an outsider.

As a victim.

3

KINGSTON

"The woman bolted from me like I had asked her to stick needles in her own eyes!"

My words are sloshed and delayed, even I can hear it in my own ears. The room began spinning some time ago, and it's only by the grace of my body weight and height that I'm still standing. Not many people can down eight shots in one minute, a dare given by one of the models, but I just did and lived to tell the tale.

For how long? That was still to be determined.

Jude smirks where he sits nursing his second beer on a retro-looking orange lounge chair. "Poppy Raymond is out of your league. Face it."

"Out of my league!? Mate, I love you, but you've gotta be more pissed than I am! No one is out of my league. I'm Kingston Bloody Phillips!"

"That's right, baby," the blonde I forgot was resting in my lap purrs in my ear.

Sweat trickles down my neck and past my shirt collar, and suddenly, my buzz turns. It's that instant where you go from happy, party smashed to annoyed at everyone and everything. I push the girl off my lap and she stumbles with a whine but marches off with a pout when I cross my leg over the other, making it clear she's not welcome to sit back down.

It's all right, I'm too legless to fuck anyway. My dick is about as useless as a penguin in Tahiti right now.

"And if you spent half as much time proving that to yourself as you do to other people, maybe you wouldn't be so lost. Or benched," my best friend mumbles.

His words hit me somewhere deep, but I'm too far gone on the liquor to analyze them. So instead, I just flick my middle finger up at him.

"Suck on this," I jeer but lose my footing as I move past him to reach for the half-empty vodka bottle in a bucket on our VIP table.

Stumbling, I try to grab hold of anything solid, but end up mowing down two toothpick models on my way to the floor. My elbow connects with the hard surface of the dance floor, and I'm lying in a puddle of spilled drinks and sweat before I realize what's happening.

"That's enough for tonight." Jude stands over me, a disapproving look on his face.

But before I can make a joke out of my fall, or protest, a surly looking bouncer drags me up, supporting my sagging weight on his shoulders and practically pulling me from the club.

"Bombshells forever!" I throw up a yell and a fist, and a swell of cheers follows me out of the after-party that moved to the club an hour ago.

There. I've left on top, even if I'm not getting on top of anyone tonight.

I'm somewhat aware as the bouncer deposits me into the back of a car and Jude slides in beside me as I rest my head against the cool window.

"King, are you all right?" He poses the question as if he's trying to ask about me past this present moment.

I pretend not to hear the note of worry in his voice. "Mate, I'm fine. Just sloshed."

"I just mean—" he tries again, and I cut him off.

"Jude, let's not talk about it now."

My brain pounds against my head with every jolt of the car, and I can feel the hangover looming over the bridge of my nose, squeezing down on it in threat of a migraine. That sober cloud of doom hangs dangerously low, and I know that soon, I'll have to think about the Pandora's box Jude is trying to open.

It's been almost nine months since I was called up to the first squad, and I haven't started one game. Riding the bench is for small league players who are brought up, or for academy players plucked for their first taste of a real match. I'm a Phillips, I should be on the field from the first whistle every single game.

Of course, the journalists and commentators haven't been kind. Lazy, clown, wash-up … you name it, it's been slung at me in the press the past couple of months. But nothing compares to the wrath of my father.

Silence is worse than any insult. He comes to the games, visits with my mum, but for four months now, has yet to utter a single word to me. I can practically feel the flesh melting off my back as I sit in the RFC player's section and he glares at me from a couple rows back.

I don't want to think about that, though. Brush it under the rug, play the hurt off with a joke or a smile. That's what I do best. A showman, that's the worst nickname they could give me. It allows the shite to slide down me, for embarrassment not to make a mark on the outside. Even if it's corroding me, eating at my organs like poison. Until it leaves me empty as a bottle that's been drunk to the last drop.

Jude helps me out of the car, says something that doesn't register, and I push him away, dragging myself toward my flat.

The familiar lobby of my building swims in my vision, with the night receptionist asking if I need any assistance. I wave her off, only wanting to crawl up to my flat and sleep this bloody night off. The elevator smells like its typical fusion of clean cotton sheets and sharp pear. Usually, I love this scent. It's crisp and reminds me of how carefully the building is taken care of. It reminds me of why I chose Charlton House to lay down my London roots.

But right now, all this smell makes me want to do is toss up the free food I ate at the after-party. A ding indicates that I've made it to the top floor, and it takes me a good three minutes to steady my hand and properly insert my key into the door of my flat, number 603.

Only a little farther before I flop myself face down on the Egyptian cotton sheets; the bed unmade from this morning. I forgot it's a Saturday, the maid won't be back until tomorrow night. Not that I'm anywhere near the state of mind to care that I'm sleeping in unwashed bedding. It's just that I'm used to people picking up after me, for my life being run by a staff of many that are as unseen as the fairies in the children's stories my nannies used to read to me.

See, I was born into privilege. Into stardom and all that comes with it.

When you're born into this world, it's almost worse than striving to make a name for yourself in it. Because everyone already knows your name, already has expectations and is secretly biding their time, hoping you fail. It's easy to fall when you're not doing so from a pedestal. But start from the top, and you shatter that much more on the way down.

Jude's words echo in my head as sleep mercifully steals over my brain. Out of my league.

I wonder, for the millionth time as I give in to the haze of alcohol-fueled dreams, if I was out of my league in this world before I even had a chance.

4
KINGSTON

The air in my lungs burns as I wheeze out a breath, trying to give the conditioning hour my all but failing miserably.

"Pick it up, Phillips. You look like my grandma over there, and she can balance better than you!" Anders Slotken, the head trainer for strength and conditioning at the RFC facilities, adds salt to my already sore invisible wounds.

I squat lower, one foot on the floor and the other raised to the height of my hip. Whoever invented these single leg squats on a BOSU ball should be hung in the town square for attempted murder. I swear, my leg went numb ten minutes ago and I'm on my way to fully dying.

"This is why he's riding the bench." Alexander Karlsson, the fair-skinned Norseman who plays right back, breathes heavy as he performs the same exercise with much more ease.

"Shut it, Alex," Jude shoots across the room, three-hundred pounds worth of dumbbell precariously balanced on his shoulders.

"Hey, you might be our prodigy, but we've been here longer

than you've been having wet dreams. Pipe down," Luigi Buosco, who starts over me at left back, scolds my best mate.

I would take up for Jude, hurl a lewd comment, especially at Luigi whose balls I love busting, but I'm in too much pain.

Slotken blows his whistle, and the room fills with huffs of relief as everyone drops to the floor in a heap of exhausted muscles. We may be professional athletes, but that only means the trainers keep coming up with punishments fit for the devil to test us.

"You're dismissed. Aside from Phillips, hit the showers."

"Fuck ..." I mutter under my breath.

Jude raises an eyebrow in my direction, as if he's asking if I want backup. We've had each other's backs since we were kids, Vance's, too. But Vance isn't here and Jude can't fight this battle with me, so I nod toward the door, silently telling him to go.

The trainer's ugly mug glowers in front of my face, and where I'd typically insert a dirty joke or a pithy comment, I shut my trap. His face says he isn't playing, and I know I've spent all of my jester pounds today.

"If you don't show some improvement, and actually apply yourself, they're going to trade you. And from what I hear, Niles is considering a championship team. Think about how embarrassed your father will be." Slotken lowers his voice for this last kernel of wisdom, as if I don't know just how much my father would hate me if that happened.

"Yes, sir." I nod my head, letting a rare vow of seriousness past my lips.

He eyes me warily, like what he just said didn't even penetrate my skull. "Just get out of my sight."

This is serious, and my head begins to spin with what-ifs. If they sell my contract to a club in the lower ranks of the British Premier League it will be a fate worse than death by conditioning.

A player doesn't come back from something like that, once you carry the stench of failure, it doesn't ever quite wash off. Maybe it would be better if that happened, if I didn't have the pressure of the world riding on my shoulders. Or maybe it would destroy me worse than this rubbish is tearing me up inside at the moment.

The thing is, I can never figure out if *I'm* actually afraid of what my life will be without football, or how *my parents* would view my life without football.

I never had a choice when it came to this sport. It's in my blood, practically lives within my DNA. Oftentimes, I wonder what I would be doing if they hadn't placed a ball at my feet at birth. I'm bloody good at it, but I'm not sure I've ever loved it. Or, if I have, I don't love it as much as someone like Jude. He bloody lives and breathes this game; it brought him from nothing to being able to care for his younger brothers when tragedy struck. Not only does he have a true passion for it, but he has more talent in his pinky than most have in their whole body.

And ... well ... I do, too. I just don't use it. When something comes easy, that's when you take it for granted the most. And if I don't have to work hard, why would I? The only thing that seems to kick my arse into gear is a trainer's boot up it, threatening to sell me and tell my father about it.

I'm the last one into the showers and am greeted by the usual bare asses and swinging knobs. No new sight for me, but it always makes me laugh like an immature twit. In what other profession do you see your colleagues naked every other day?

The guys are waxing poetic on this week's latest hookups, and I cut into the conversation, trying to get my mind off all the deep bullshit Slotken just brought up.

"Poppy Raymond, you know anything about her?" I direct this at Luigi.

Alex flashes a glare at his veteran teammate, warning him

not to answer the question. It was well-known that Luigi cheated on his wife regularly, especially with girls who weren't actually age appropriate to his elderly thirty-two. That kind of number was basically a death sentence on your career in football.

"Don't you dare. I don't want to know if you slept with that girl, basically young enough to be your daughter. And you don't want anyone, especially your wife, to hear you confess to that either." Alex points a finger at him and then exits the showers.

But Luigi, per usual, doesn't listen to what's good for him. His eyes scan the showers, assessing who is in the room, and then he talks out of the side of his mouth.

"Rumor is, she doesn't put out for anyone. Never takes anyone home, goes solo to most industry events. So, it's said that she's either a complete prude or an undercover slag. I ... I vote for the latter. No woman who looks like that, with how long she's been in this world, isn't a total freak in the sheets."

Jude just rolls his eyes. "So, all you know is whispers and rumors? Great, we're really running on credible information here. Can you drop this? The girl has a biting tongue, but she's voiced her distaste. Go pick on someone your own sleaze size."

It's directed at me, but I'm still hanging on Luigi's every word. "So, you're saying there could be an in?"

The Italian arsehole shrugs. "It won't be easy."

That makes me square my shoulders because as I said, why work at anything that comes easy?

"Good thing hard is my middle name." I waggle my eyebrows and a couple of the blokes on the squad snort.

We exit the showers, moving to our individual lockers.

"No, easy is your middle name. When it comes to matches, work, money ... but especially women. You love easy women. Stick to them." Jude claps me on the shoulder.

"Says the man who groveled at a woman's feet the minute she became a challenge," I mutter, and he glares at me.

Nothing seems to come easy these days. Not football, and not women.

Well, that isn't entirely true, I'm just feeling pity for myself and taking it to the nth degree. In reality, I could call up any fit bird in London and she'd be over to my flat, on her knees, in seconds. There was available pussy everywhere, and it was mine for the taking.

But ever since Poppy Raymond turned me down, I'm like a dog with a bone. Or a dog with an itch I can't scratch. Either way, I'm a bloody horny animal with rocks that I can't get off. I even slept with one of those D-list reality show girls last night, and it got pretty wild. Though not enough to make me forget one sassy brunette with a chip on her shoulder.

Out of my league? Yeah, right. If anything, Poppy and I are perfect equals. The poster children for our given crafts, and bloody hell, we'd make one dishy pair. So what the hell is wrong with her? If she's not a lesbian, like I'd guessed all those months ago, and she wasn't in a relationship ...

I was going to bet on Luigi's intel. Or at least, pray like bloody hell she wasn't some devout prude.

There was nothing worse than a face like that being wasted on something as bloody useless as abstinence.

5

POPPY

"*Poppy! This way!*"

"*Over here, Poppy, look over here!*"

"*Ms. Raymond, smile! Give it to us!*"

The photographers shout my name, a frenzied fever sweeping over the junket of them from where they stand on the other side of a metal barricade.

I give it to them, as they say, pouting appropriately and then dazzling them with a mega-watt smile. My body moves in its typical poses, the one the thousand-dollar-an-hour consultant taught me when I was a gangly, awkward teenager just breaking into the modeling industry.

It's the dance we do, the one to stay in the spotlight. The slow steps in a burning room, eventually bringing us all the way to the ground, to ashes. It scalds a little every day, not enough to notice at first, only a layer of skin. But eventually, give too many pounds of flesh you can't get back, and you're left with nothing at all. Just a hollowed-out shell of the person you used to be.

As soon as I exit the red carpet, I steel my nerves for the real shark pool. It's not the photographers and the press junkets you need to be scared of, it's the vicious carnivores inside this awards show that are toxic. The United Kingdom Television Awards are a sought after invitation every year, and for this awards show, the Gallileo fashion house wanted me to wear their signature dress of the season. There was no way I could say no.

The dress is a column of shimmering sparkles, the color of the sea when it rolls and crests on the beaches of the Maldives. No really, that's what the designer who sketched it out told me was her inspiration. It's an ombre, skin-tight frock that rests on my bust, no straps, and cascades to the floor. The six-inch silver heels I have on can't even be seen, but they make me impossibly tall.

Heads begin to turn as I make my way through the room, a couple of celebrities I've encountered in the past stopping to say hello or admire my ensemble. Some of the girls I've worked jobs with or actors I've done magazine spreads with, halt my progress to chat and rub elbows. If we can all appear in photos together, they'll end up on some entertainment website and being seen with this person or that person raises your clout. It's all a game.

My game tonight? Make it to the bar with the least amount of interactions under my belt. I want a healthy amount of champagne coursing through my system before I have to be seated at my table. I shimmy my way through the crowd, already craving the taste of bubbles on my tongue. As soon as my veins succumb to the floating feeling of a buzz, this will be easier.

Slapping my palm on the bar, the bartender's attention homes in on me and I order. Perks of being extra shiny in a room of already-sparkling people.

"Well, hello, gorgeous."

The deep vibrato tone licks up my spine. He has one of those voices that can completely undress you, causing a stir of arousal deep in your belly, even if you're fully clothed in a room of people. The feeling is so foreign to me because, of course, I've read about this kind of thing, or watched it acted out in a movie, but men never affect me this way. Quite the opposite; when a man of a certain caliber, like those in this room, talks to me with anything that signals sexual interest it makes my blood run cold.

But I know who this voice belongs to, and it's why I'm extra miffed about the way it warms everything south of my belly button.

"Hm, seems we haven't yet gotten the clue." I throw a sneering smile Kingston's way.

He's too dapper in his jet-black tuxedo, that mop of sandy blond hair slicked back. It makes him look like James Dean ... or like he has womanizer written all over him.

"And what clue would that be? That you detest me? Oh no, love, I've gotten that loud and clear. Seems I just don't care." Those emerald eyes spark with the wit from his banter.

A flute appears in front of me and I suck down half the liquid, the carbonation tickling my nose. "How caveman of you."

"Tell me a secret." He winks, holding a brandy snifter to his mouth. "Any secret. I want to understand the enigma that is Poppy Raymond."

Now he's just raving mad if he thinks I'm going to do anything of the sort. "You really are off your trolley. Why the bloody hell do you think I'd share any kind of secret with the likes of you? You couldn't handle this enigma."

My glass is midway to my lips when I spot him.

Everything in the room freezes from my vantage point. The chatter, the music, the glitz of the lights and the waitstaff catering to every guest's every whim. In my ears, a whooshing sound starts, like I'm literally being pulled under a current and the water is drowning my senses.

I knew this was a possibility. There always is when I agree to attend one of these events. I'd talked myself through the scenarios, but it seems that hasn't worked in the slightest.

It all hits me in one nauseating wave, and I almost double

over with the horrific proximity of him. He doesn't see me, has some rail-thin girl on his arm—and I do mean girl. She can't be a day over sixteen. With his dark hair peppered with gray, sagging tan skin and those piercing blue eyes that haunt my dreams ...

It all has me turning, running.

Because I can't stay here. There is no way I can sit in the same ballroom as him and not be mentally bloody dismantled. My mind will go into a tailspin, my body will collapse into the fits of a nervous breakdown.

No one will notice if I leave now before the tables are seated. Sure, someone might assume I had too many drinks during the cocktail hour, or that I'm off puking my guts out from bulimia in the bathroom. But who cares? Let them. It's loads better than the actual truth getting out.

"Poppy?" Vaguely, I hear my name called out as I retreat.

My vision blurs as I run from the room, and as I reach the sidewalk, flashbulbs begin to dot everything I see. The car my publicist ordered must be out here somewhere, and when I spot a large black sedan, I know it's my escape option.

Collapsing into the back seat, my limbs are so knackered from the deflating of adrenaline and burst of exercise, that I slump against the leather, trying to catch my breath.

That's when the door on the other side of the back seat swings open, and Kingston folds his long limbs inside.

6

POPPY

"Get the fuck out of my car!" I screech at him, incensed.

I haven't allowed a man this close to me, in such an enclosed space, in years. And while the usual alarm bells aren't triggering in my head, I am brutally aware of his masculine proximity to my body. The fact that his knee is almost touching mine, and that he plans to keep it that way for however long it takes to reach his end destination for the night, is making my heart go bonkers.

"This is my Uber, babe. So you can either stay, which I'd be more than happy with, or you can go. Your choice, doll face."

The nickname makes me cringe. "You're disgusting. And who in your position in life takes Uber?"

I stare at the driver of the black Escalade, who I now realize is a thirty-something girl who looks vaguely like Kristen Bell. Before I got in, I thought this was the town car that had been ordered for me, and she hadn't even bothered to ask my name or suggest that she wasn't a hired service. Which only demonstrates how dangerous the car-ordering service is.

"It's much cheaper than a car service, and you meet some interesting people in these things." The arsehole shrugs, looking too cute and devilish at the same time, which until now I didn't realize was possible.

"I'll tell them that when they ask me for a quote for your obituary. You know, when you're murdered." I roll my eyes.

"If you have to explain the pithy comment, it wasn't really that pithy." Kingston looks so chuffed, I want to sock him in the mouth.

"Are you all going to the same location?" Kristen Bell-looka-like asks in a bored tone.

"Yes, we are!" Kingston answers cheerfully, cutting off my protest.

"You don't even know where I'm going!" I hiss at him, thoroughly fuming when he moves over enough in the roomy back seat so that his tuxedo-clad knee is pressed against the sequined skirt of my dress. I can feel the heat through the fabric.

Damn this wonky heart and its irrational beating.

"You looked practically lurgy back there. Either you saw a ghost, or snuck a few too many tuna tartars before the show. I wanted to make sure you are okay." His voice takes on a tone of concern, and I give him my full gaze.

For a moment, we stare at each other, and I think I see something deeper than the jester's costume he shows to the world.

But then he speaks. "It's not every day a woman runs away from me. I needed to know why."

That has me rolling my eyes. "So it wasn't about if I was ill or not. You just wanted to bandage your wounded pride."

"And now you're riding home with me. So it worked, didn't it?" His handsome face creases into a pleased grin.

Turning my head toward the window, I refuse to give him any more leverage. There was something about that beat of a moment that had just passed between us, and it both frightened and intrigued me. I can't allow the latter feeling to get the best of my good sense.

When the car pulls up to Charlton House, I glance across the car at the building my flat resides in.

Catching a glimpse of Kingston's chiseled face, I notice the look he wears is one of curious, confused amusement. The streaks of moonlight that fall into the back seat of the car light up his green eyes, which dance with some expression I can't place.

"Don't think that because you followed me back to my flat, I'm allowing you up. In fact, I'm calling security if you even step foot in the lobby." I turn my nose up in his direction, then barrel out of the car, heading with purpose up the steps and through the glass entrance doors.

Except as my heels clatter on the marble, a second set of heavier steps join them.

My eyes must be pure hatred as I whip my head around. "What the hell do you think you're doing?"

"Good evening, Mr. Phillips." A new receptionist, one I don't recognize as working the after-midnight shift, greets Kingston with a nod. And then, as if forgetting me, she squeaks out, "Miss Raymond, have a good night."

"Have a good night, Janina." His football pitch-green eyes wink in her direction.

What the bloody hell is going on? Suspicion, deft and deadly as a python, curls in my stomach, but I refuse to let my nonchalant mask slip. Not that I haven't already bugged out on him multiple times, but I'll be damned if he thinks I am going to play twenty questions with him about how he knows the lobby staff in my building.

I wouldn't be surprised if he was shagging six different women in this building. Ah yes, that was how they knew him, he must be a frequent nighttime visitor.

Clacking along the gleaming floors, I can feel the blood pulsing in my ears. The closer I get to the bank of lifts, the more furious I get that Kingston Phillips is tailing me like a corgi following Queen Elizabeth. My index finger decisively calls for the lift, and I tap my heel on the floor, unconsciously vibrating with rage.

Out of the corner of my eye, I see the satisfied smirk on his full, raspberry-colored mouth. What kind of man has such captivating lips? You can barely keep your eyes off them if you stare at him straight on, and it's biting at me even more than his presence. What gives this arse the license to be so damn gorgeous?

"After you." He ushers me in as the chime of the lift signals the opening of its doors.

"Leave. Now. Or I'll call the police," I spit, as if the words are nasty swears.

"Oh, I don't think that will be necessary, love."

And just as frustratingly as he slid into my car, he slides a key to the penthouse floor out of his pocket and inserts it in the specially designed notch. That only residents of the top floor of Charlton House are given access to.

"What … how …" I'm truly too stunned to speak.

Kingston pushes the button for the floor, the lift begins to rise, and he dazzles me with a cocky grin. "Nice to meet you, *neighbor*."

No. *No*. Bloody hell on toast … *NO*. "You're joking."

"Afraid not, gorgeous. But I have to say, I'm truly upset we didn't realize this sooner. Think of all the sleepovers we've missed out on."

"In your dreams." The huff comes out of my mouth, but I'm still too shocked to come up with anything wittier.

"Oh, Poppy, if you only knew the dreams I have about you."

The way Kingston's voice teems with innuendo, it's impossible not to meet his eye. And when I do … good lord. There is a reason why vulnerable women always succumb to dishy men in lifts in movies or on TV shows. The enclosed space, the sexual tension bouncing off the walls. There is nowhere for it to go but straight into the most sensitive spot between my thighs. Kingston's gaze grows steamier, and his tongue darts out to do a slow sweep of his bottom lip. It's erotic, and my breath catches in my lungs.

He steps forward, just a hair's breadth but enough for each of our bodies to stir restlessly. I feel my nipples harden, and though I've spent the last hour ridiculing him I don't take a step back at his advance. My mind whirls from the realization of it.

And then the lift doors chime, opening up to the gleaming hallway of the penthouse level. *Our* hallway.

Kingston steps out first, walking backward and maintaining eye contact with me, a small smirk dusting his lips. I'm entranced, slowly following him in a haze, though the half glass of champagne I drank didn't even touch my raw nerves. His big, lean body passes my door, his feet shuffling to a stop in front of the alcove of flat number 603.

"Good night, Poppy," he says quietly, the electricity crackling between us.

Then, in the most unique of twists, the playboy of London himself opens his front door, walks through it, and then shuts it tight.

I'm left standing in our shared hallway, wondering how in God's name I'm going to live here now that I know Kingston Phillips is my neighbor.

7

KINGSTON

I had her, right there in my sights, finger on the trigger ...

And I couldn't follow through.

What the hell happened in that lift last night?

My mind wanders to the magnetic field pulling me toward Poppy in our shared rides last night, both in the car and in our building's lift. She was the picture of perfection last night; not even in my wettest of dreams would my fantasy girl come close to her in that sparkling dress she wore. And how the entire back of the frock was cut out, resting scintillatingly right over the top of her tailbone? Christ, I could die and go to heaven just staring at that spot long enough.

Of course, I am sexually attracted to her, any man with two eyes is. But that doesn't explain why I didn't kiss her? Why I refrained from making my move, especially when it appeared I'd finally tamed her in the lift. Her mood toward me had shifted, I could feel it. I even took a step toward her, and I knew the moment she didn't retreat that I could have held her naked body in my arms.

Something in my brain just wouldn't let me follow my most

base instincts. That never bloody happened. And now it was fucking killing me that I didn't know why.

"King, will you pay attention? Jesus, get on the other side of Aria," Vance snaps at me, pointing to the other side of the giant white photo backdrop.

I do as I'm told, navigating past the other models or friends of Jude's to stand next to his girlfriend.

"One too many last night?" She smirks, but I see the concern in her eyes.

"Nothing you have to worry about, Pipes." I rub my shoulder against hers, using the nickname I started calling her after her first album won a Grammy.

As the camera shutter clicks in our direction, we both put on our faux competitive faces.

We're all modeling Jude's new active wear line, set to release into stores in about a month or so. And who better to show off his labor of love than his famous friends. Plus, we're all doing it for free. Though Aria gets sexual favors afterward and that seems unfair; I even told my best friend so. He then smacked me in the stomach with the backside of his hand and told me to get to work.

I had to hand it to him; the line is posh. A lot of sleek black and navy blues, or stark whites. Smart designs, sweat-proof material, and the Jude Davies kiss of approval ... yeah, this line is going to sell like hotcakes. My mate was capitalizing on his worth, and he was brilliant to do so.

"All right, we're going to get some solo shots of Jude now in the various looks, so you all can hit craft services," the photographer tells us, and Aria, Vance, and I step off the giant backdrop.

"I'm bloody starving." Vance rubs his abs, and I'm not surprised.

"You're always starving, big guy." I slap a hand on his shoulder, which is modeled after the Hulk's muscle tone.

Vance's eyebrows bow in, showcasing his annoyance. "Yeah, well, I actually follow my training schedule, so it's no wonder I'm burning much more energy and calories than you."

"Oh, jab at my laziness, how original." I roll my eyes but am glad for the verbal sparring.

I've missed Vance, and it guts me to see him still stuck at Rogue Academy without us. But until Remus Bayern, RFC's star keeper, either leaves for another team or gets injured ... well, he's shite out of luck. It's a shit hand, but that's the luck of the draw when you play the keeper position. Only so many of those spots to go around, and if you happen to reach the peak of your talent in an off year, it's just the misfortune of bad timing. Nothing can be done.

I can tell it's getting to the bloke, though. He seems more tense than usual and that's saying something.

"I've missed you two." Aria grins, walking in step with us as we approach a table loaded with sandwiches, fruit, cookies, and many other delicacies.

"Pssh, okay, Miss World Tour. You got famous and forgot all about us. Rubbing elbows with Adele and Katy Perry ... give me a break. Someday, when the reporters ask, I'll tell them I knew the sweet girl from Clavering."

Aria shoots me a glare. "I was never sweet, and look who's talking, Mr. Playboy of Piccadilly. I'm pretty sure you've slept with more pop stars than I've toured with."

I raise a hand. "Guilty."

They both roll their eyes, then Vance's phone rings. A cloud of fury flashes over his face so lightning fast, I'm tempted to back up. I've only seen Vance lose his temper two times ... and in both of those instances, he landed himself in the Clavering town jail. If anyone learns anything from me, it's to stay away from that bloke when he's angry.

"Excuse me." His voice is gruff as he stalks away, jabbing an angry finger onto the screen of his mobile.

"What was that all about?" Aria wonders aloud.

I shrug. "Not sure, but don't ask him. You'll end up with a broken arm."

"You boys don't scare me." She folds her arms as I reach for an apple.

"Pipes, you tamed Jude; Vance and I are a whole other level of cocked up."

"Speaking of cocking up, what's going on with you? Jude says you were late to practice the other day, and almost missed the cutoff time for a match day warm up? Come on, Kingston, you're better than that."

We've become close, Aria and me. I think it's because we see the weakness we feel inside, mirrored in each other. We come from vastly different backgrounds, but unlike Jude, we don't innately believe in the talent we possess. It's a struggle to not place uncertainty on our individual passions, me with football and Aria with singing. Our friendship is one comprised of banter and joking, but also of comfort and understanding.

"Yeah, yeah, I overslept with a certain socialite." I try to brush off her worry with a smile and a dance—my usual joker's routine.

But, as usual, that doesn't work with Aria. We're alone near the craft services table, and she ushers me over to a table and chairs out of the way of the photo shoot action.

I sit, only because I respect her far too much to ditch her, but know she's about to grill me.

"Don't try to feed me that codswallop, it won't work. I'm in love with your best mate, so I'm immune to your charm. Unfortunately, I can see through your super power. So, come on, out with it. What's going on?"

Bugger, she's relentless this tiny force of determination. No wonder Jude fancies her so much.

"There have been rumblings about selling me to a lower league team. Something about my attitude, or my work ethic, or some other shite I don't care to pay attention to."

"Kingston ..." Aria clucks her tongue.

"I know, I know, I have to try harder. I don't want to leave RFC, at least not to play anywhere else. It's the best club in London, where would I possibly go if not there? It's just ... I don't know if I love it."

Her eyes tell me she knows the answer, but she asks a different question anyway. "The club?"

"The game."

Aria nods wisely, as if she's always suspected this. "Just because we're good at something, doesn't mean we have to like it. I was a damn good seamstress, but ask me if I'd ever go back to sewing kits? Even for a million dollars, I'd say hell no. For you, it's the toughest position to be put in. This is your legacy ... admitting that you don't want it is a harder feat than what most people face."

The photo shoot continues in the background of our conversation, and I direct my gaze toward it to soften the blow of the depths Aria and I have waded into. She may be cajoling me into having this talk, but it doesn't mean I have to make eye contact.

"It's not, though. You supported your family on your back at eighteen, while your father went through cancer treatments. Jude lost his parents, bloody hell he raises his younger brothers. All I have to do is play football and live off my mum and dad's names and money. If I walked away from that, everyone would call me a dumb wanker."

"Just because you had a leg up at the starting line doesn't mean you're contractually obligated to follow the path. You don't have to go through some horrible tragedy to want a different life for yourself. If you don't love football, don't play the game. But if you do love it, commit to it, Kingston. Stop wavering. Put your all into it, or don't do it at all. You'll be miserable as long as you keep this halfsies shite up. And I don't want you to be miserable. A smarmy arse, yes. But a clearly conflicted, unhappy one? No. None of us want that for you."

Blimey, she'd gone and called my bluff pretty accurately.

"Thanks, Pipes. I appreciate you looking out for me," I tell her in a moment of full seriousness, which is rare for me.

Because, of course, she's right. I haven't been truly happy in … bloody hell, probably my entire life. I need to figure out how much of what I do in my life is actually for me. And if it is, then even I can admit I need to grow a pair and go after it.

We both observe Jude posing for the camera, trying his best to impersonate Ben Stiller in *Zoolander*. I crack a smile because he's faking the edgy look in a warehouse in Chelsea while someone pats makeup onto his forehead every other take. It's pretty humorous.

"I met my new neighbor the other day," I throw out there, interrupting the silence between Aria and me.

"Don't tell me you had another noise complaint. You're going to get kicked out of the building, Kingston!" But Aria is laughing as she says it.

With a shake of my head, I deliver the news. "Nope, no noise complaint. Just a lift ride littered with sexual tension. Poppy Raymond. She bought the flat next door."

"No! The gorgeous Amazon who bit your head off at that club?" She snorts in laughter. "That is some kind of karma. The one woman who doesn't want to go anywhere near your bed is now the closest bird to it."

Maybe she's right, karma was coming to take a chunk out of my arse.

The Lion Heart

"She is gorgeous, isn't she?" I murmur, almost to myself. "Hell of a mouth on her, too."

"You're in love with her." Aria pokes a finger into my bicep.

A piece of the apple lodges in my throat and I spasm into a coughing fit.

"Blimey, you almost killed me. Don't use that word in my presence again, I think I'm allergic to it," I scold her.

Aria nods her head smugly in my direction. "Oh, you'll see. This girl is going to be the end of Kingston Phillips. I can see it already."

8

POPPY

London in late spring is unlike any place on earth.

It's warm enough to leave your coat or sweater at home, and the sun begins to reappear for the first time in months. There are flowers blooming in the trees, restaurants begin to pull their tables back out onto the pavement, and Londoners flock to the parks, sunning themselves while eating to-go sandwiches from Pret or Tesco.

My bank account may be padded with pounds, but there is no better lunch than a Tesco two-pound meal deal. I didn't grow up with a silver spoon in my mouth, so I know how satisfying a cheap combo can be to both the mind and the stomach.

Back to my point, though ... London in spring smelled of hope and a new beginning, and it was addicting. Which was why I'd forgone the car that the agency had sent to pick me up from my photo shoot, some swimwear line that was set to debut. I much preferred walking this time of year, even if my flat was two-and-a-half kilometers from the studio.

I'm admiring the architecture of the brownstones lining a clean-swept street when my mobile rings.

Fishing it out of my violet leather Chanel bag, my sister's

name flashes on the screen. I exhale a measured breath through my nose, because this conversation is not going to leave me with cheery warm feelings. My family only calls when they want or need something. I click the green button to pick up the call and press it to my ear.

"Poppy, I'm just wondering if you'll be coming home for the bridal shower? I'm doing the seating chart and need your RSVP."

Not even a "Cheerio," or a "How are you doing?"

I've already told her twice that, yes, I'll be there. I've cleared my schedule for two entire days, which for me during fashion week season is terribly difficult. But I did it, and she knows that. Though, of course, she wants to make me feel bad or jealous or inferior, so she's asking again.

Sometimes I can't reconcile the Tabitha of this age with the one of old. My sister and I used to be close; sneaking sticks of gum under the pew benches, walking home the long way from school, building flashlight forts under our blankets at night and telling each other ghost stories. She is only two years older than I am, but we'd always been each other's confidants.

"Yes, like I told you, I will be at your shower. Is there anything you need help with? Anything I can contribute?" I say politely because that's what a good sister would do.

I can practically hear her sneer from the other end of the call. "No, that won't be necessary. It may be quaint compared to your standards, but we won't be spending nearly as much as you might budget for a party."

As if I threw lavish events for myself costing something in the millions. How could my own flesh and blood turn their noses up at how successful I am? It seemed even crueler than a family who rides the coattails of their wealthy relatives.

But I brush off her frigid comments because she *is* my sister. I want to be a part of her big day, and I learned very quickly in this industry that you create your own life. You can accept people as they are, keep them around, cut them out of your life ... but whatever you do, make sure you're building the version of you that you aspire to be. Other people won't influence that if you don't let them, but you can be a bigger, better person and give them the chance and the hope that they'll improve the way you want them to.

And that's how I feel when it comes to my sister.

"How is Mom doing?" I ask Tabitha, curious as to how everything has shaken out there in the last year.

Since, well ... since my perfectly conservative housewife of a mother found out that my practically pastoral father had an affair with their close church friend. As if I didn't have enough issues when it came to men, now I had to deal with the fallout of my father, whom I had always thought was at least decent if not harshly devout in his beliefs, destroying any little hope I had left in the male species.

It happened six months ago, and it was the one and only time my mother had even remotely let me see into her emotional side. She called me, sobbing quietly, to tell me the news. In that moment, my heart had shattered. My parents have a traditional, Christian marriage. She has been subservient to my father, aiming to please him every day since the day they traded rings on the altar. It wasn't fair that she should have to go through this, no matter how fractured my relationship is with her.

There's only so much of my soul left after what had happened to me all those years ago. Hearing of my father's infidelities ... that gutted me. Say what you want about him, but I'd at least thought he was one of the good ones. Having to face the reality of a positive male role model in my life being just as rubbish as the rest ... it stole a piece of my remaining soul.

"She's already feeling better about it. Has forgiven Daddy

and they've prayed on it. The devil, he got to him. But sin can be absolved, with the right amount of church time and family strength. You should really try to come home, Poppy. They'd both love to see you in this time of great need."

Blimey, she sounds like a nun. I can't believe this is the same sister who once taught me how to sneak *Cosmopolitan* magazine into the lining of my backpack so that Mum wouldn't find it when we got home from school.

"I'll be home for the shower, Tabitha. But you should know, I'm not going to pray about it." I've always stayed firm in my stance that I didn't share their beliefs.

Growing up, church was our second home. It was expected we'd attend Sunday services, catechism school during the week, be involved in youth group. I had no choice but to listen to the priest's words or opinions; the Bible was my nightly reading. I didn't question its lessons or what I was being fed until much later.

But when I did, I blew the hypnotism hat my parents placed upon my head clear off. I didn't believe any of that codswallop anymore. How could I? What kind of God would allow unspeakable things to happen to a fourteen-year-old girl? And, not that it happened at the hands of a priest or clergyman, what kind of church covered up the assault of its parishioners?

I couldn't justify that enough against the things they preached, so I halted my religious activities altogether.

"I can't have this fight, again. Goodbye, Poppy," Tabitha clips into the phone, and then the line goes dead.

Just as well, it wouldn't have ended with either of us changing our stance. As I enter the lobby of my building, having walked all the way home while on the phone, I'm reminded of just how necessary it is to stay away from my neighbor. Because if men like my father can't even be trusted, then the arrogant football player next door certainly can't be.

Kingston Phillips reminds me of every smarmy bloke whose only goal in life is to get into a woman's pants. And I don't mean just one woman's knickers. No, this playboy's mission is to sleep his way round the entire country of England, and then move on to the other countries of Europe. Perhaps branch out to the States. He is my father, multiplied by good looks and fat pockets. Kingston is an elite, grew up in the cushiest of worlds and has the smug attitude to prove it. He believes he's untouchable, that the word no doesn't exist where he's concerned. And he works it all with an air of humor, that's what makes women think he's approachable. But, I know, it's what makes him that much more dangerous.

So, I'll deploy my usual tactics, tenfold. I use my quips, my sass, and my backtalk to throw anyone off the scent. Because if I can put on a front like I don't care about them, or that I'm indifferent to almost any situation I'm in … it's far better than anyone discovering what's really in my head. That on the inside, I'm dying a slow death. That internally, I'm empty and cold, the feelings that once began blossoming there were stolen from me five years ago by someone who knew better.

9

KINGSTON

I don't run into Poppy on our penthouse floor until a week and a half after our shared lift ride.

The lift doors open and immediately, I spot a pair of legs shuffling back and forth, the top half of the person obscured.

Obviously, I know exactly whose gorgeous poles those are, especially since I found out an actual goddess was occupying the flat next door.

Grocer's bags are piled high in Poppy's arms, teetering precariously in the air, about to tumble to the ground. She's fumbling with her keys, trying to get them in the lock to open the door, and everything is about to come crashing down when she takes an unexpected side step.

"Woah!" I dart forward, looping one arm around her waist and the other around the loaded paper bags.

"Blimey! You scared me!" she yelps but stays still in my embrace.

It's probably not so she can be close to me, but so she can save the half a watermelon dangerously close to splattering into pieces on the plush carpet of our shared hallway. Still, I savor the half a second that I'm allowed to get close to her. Her skin is warmer than I anticipated, like she's been sunning on a beach in the Grecian islands. Smells like it too, some mixture of coconut and shea butter tickles my nostrils and I want to inhale that scent for the rest of my life. From afar, Poppy appears to be all hard angles and edgy beauty. But holding her, I feel the dips and crevices of her figure, the padding of her bum against my front and the teasing curve of her neck where my mouth sits just inches from.

"But I saved you. So, I think in the end, it was worth it." Easily, I pluck three of the bags out of her arms, leaving her with a lighter and much more manageable trip.

"I can handle it on my own." She swipes at me to take back her parcels, but I swerve, avoiding her reach.

Poppy huffs, instead, turning her attention back to the lock. The stubborn bird, she *really* doesn't enjoy my company.

"Don't you have people who stock these things for you? I come home and food appears in my refrigerator or pantry. We're rich, Poppy, these are things we don't *have* to do," I point out as she finally manages to get her front door open.

She sends those eyes, the color of a sun-drenched blue sky, rolling toward the ceiling. "You really have never done one bit of work in your life, have you? Have you ever even stepped foot inside a Waitrose? How about, *gasp*, a Tesco?"

I wrinkle my nose. "No, why would I? Someone's always done it for me."

"You're really so out of touch with the world, it's *mad*. For your information, I enjoy going to the market. I enjoy picking out my food and then bringing it home to cook it. There is something satisfying about organizing the pantry or lining up my cans of ginger ale in the fridge. Completing household chores gives one a sense of purpose, you should try it sometime."

"Thanks, but I think I'll pass." I push farther into her flat.

She hasn't extended an invitation, but I figure I saved her carton of eggs from imminent doom, so I've earned the right.

Doing a sweep of her flat, I notice it has a similar layout as my own. Open concept, with three steps down to the sunken living room across from the front door. Traditionally framed, white floor-to-ceiling windows with a view out onto the London cityscape along the back wall. The kitchen on the right, with a full bath immediately next to me, and I know from just glancing down it that the short hallway on the left contains doors to the master bedroom, spare, and den-type room which I've converted into a film room for myself. I claim it's for match-day rewatches and studying, but the only thing I've actually screened are all the *Die Hard* movies.

Aside from the layout, though, the similarities are few and far between. While I knocked out all the old English finishes and transformed my flat into a modern piece of bachelor art, Poppy has opted to keep them. Her space is all cozy neutral paints with touches of soft pink and big overstuffed furniture that looks brilliant to take an afternoon snooze on. The theme, as I've been taught by my interior-designer mum, is antique chic … an updated, millennial version of traditional British decorating. It's what Kate Middleton's house probably looks like, if I had to venture a guess.

Her kitchen, as she promised, looks like it's actually been used. There is a large white ceramic pitcher on the counter that looks to be filled with homemade iced tea, a bowl of fresh apples on the island, and a kettle on the stove hand-painted with tiny pink flowers. It's the kind of piece that someone else probably pays a pretty pound for, but I have a feeling this one is passed down for generations.

That odd thought makes me come to the conclusion that I know very little about Poppy and being in her home makes me want to peel back the layers.

"Who said you could come in here?" She gives a little start when she spins around, having just put her cold items into the fridge.

"I was helping you bring in groceries, remember?" I smile, trying to keep the charm and tease out of it.

My usual tactics don't work to attract Poppy, so I'm going to try a new approach. Being ... *nice*. That sounds totally lame, and maybe I've gone mental, but if the end goal is still to get her naked beneath me, does it really matter?

The way her eyes go all shifty as she stands just feet away from me, on the other side of the island, makes me think about what Luigi said about her. Is she really a prude, or just exceptionally frigid? Maybe there is a man in her life, one she doesn't make public. Is that why she's acting like I may just set her living room ablaze?

"And now I'm ... what? Supposed to offer you a cup of tea?" The words seem to cause her physical pain as she directs them at me.

I can't see those gorgeous, toned, tanned legs behind the counter, but I can tell Poppy is shifting from foot to foot. The world's favorite model is dressed down today, in a pair of worn-in blue jeans and a casual gray T-shirt. Her face is free of the paint and sorcery that transforms women, and all of those long chocolate waves are spilling over her shoulders. Something in my chest wriggles free, and I'm hit with a burst of realization that I'd prefer seeing her with her hair let down, so to speak, than in a glitzy cocktail dress any day.

Who the hell have I suddenly turned into? I give my head a tiny shake, to clear it, and remember my mission; get in her knickers.

"I'll take that, or sexual favors. Either repayment is fine with me." I take it upon myself to walk to a particularly cozy looking chair and flop down on it.

"Does this really work for you?" She points a red fingernail in my direction, her nose wrinkling in distaste.

"Being ridiculously good-looking and curling my finger at whatever woman I want?" I shrug. "Yes, typically."

Poppy sighs in annoyance. "The women of this world ... no standards."

"What are your standards? Come on, I'm dying to know. If I'm not good enough for the number one Boudoir Bombshell, who is?"

She busies herself with the kettle, filling it with water and adding four tea bags and a dollop of sugar before even putting it on the stove. It's the way one of my favorite nannies used to fix tea. A memory of my mother calling it a backward method and correcting the employee comes floating back to me. I always did prefer my tea that way rather than soaking the herbs and leaves in already boiling water.

"Why, so you can turn yourself into Prince Charming? I'll give you a heads-up, it's not going to work." The muscles in the slim column of her back work as she moves around the kitchen.

I follow her, all of her grace and strength hypnotizing me. "Nah, I know I play the role of the scoundrel. No need to tell me that. But maybe I can be your wingman. Get you a good shag. How about it?"

"You really are just a randy twit, aren't you?" She laughs, almost as if it's with me rather than against me.

"And proud of it." I slap a hand to my heart, as if I'm pledging allegiance to the dirty rotten playboy she's found me out to be.

Poppy sighs and turns around, having no more busy work to distract her from me sitting in her living room. Her long legs eat up the space between us, and she folds them underneath her on the white linen sofa she sinks down onto.

"Honestly, I'm too busy most of the time to think about

finding a nice bloke. Or what he'd even look like. But I suppose, if I had to dream one up ..."

She taps one of those red fingernails to her chin and I wish I could bite the tip of it, gently, with my teeth. This is probably one of the only times I've ever been alone with a woman, in *her* home, completely sober. Much less, in the middle of the day. I've had many women, but none of them have ever been more than a one-night fling ... if I even let them stay until the morning.

Bickering with Poppy, sitting here in her space, it's kind of ... nice. Bloody hell, how lame is that?

"He'd be tall because he can't be shorter than me."

I hold one finger in the air. "First checkmark for me. Go on, I want to see how many of your boxes I tick off."

If she notices that I give a little side of eyebrow waggle with my innuendo, she doesn't say anything.

Though she does actually seem to consider my question. "A job, he has to have a good one. One he's passionate about because I love my job and won't date someone who doesn't feel the same way about their career. And I'm busy; I don't have time to entertain some lazy bugger. He ought to be kind and supportive, a man who can take charge but also is comfortable letting me lead. And I don't want someone who takes themselves so seriously, like a lot of the men I encounter do."

"Hmm, this is really turning out to be eye-opening. Seems the perfect man is sitting in front of you." I wave my hands up and down my body, as if to demonstrate that I'm available on a silver platter.

Poppy lets out an amused sigh. "Oh, Kingston. I do have to admire your tenacity. It's still a no, though."

As she rises to shut off the stove and remove the whistling kettle, I follow her. This conversation was just getting interesting, and now she wants to extinguish it by pouring hot tea all over it.

"What about his ability to pleasure you? To make you scream in ecstasy? How about an orgasm quota he has to hit?"

"Kingston, stop ..." Her voice is doing that haughty deflection thing I've come to recognize.

She does this when she's shy, or uncomfortable. And, as is my nature, I barrel right through it. I'm moving closer to her, invading her space, and she sets the teapot down, trying to maneuver away. The counter and island have her blocked in. With nowhere to run, she has to answer my questions.

"Okay, fine. I'll leave the sex talk for another day. But how about kissing? Does he have to satisfy a minimum amount of kisses a day? Maybe just one when he leaves for work?"

Those aqua pools shift nervously, and something I don't quite know how to read appears in her irises for a split second. It sends a jolt right through me.

I'm so close to her right now, that teasing scent of coconut wafts over me. She's so beautiful, blinking up at me like some kind of innocent, naïve animal. This encounter has ripped away all of her acerbic words and biting attitude. Underneath the facade, Poppy Raymond is just a young girl who ...

Wait one bloody minute ...

My voice is a whisper of pure shock when I ask my next question. "Have you ever been kissed?"

10

POPPY

"Have you ever been kissed?"

He poses the question as if the answer is simple. For most people, it would be. But for me ... I'm not even quite sure how to answer that.

Have I ever felt the rush of excitement at the thought of a boy pressing his lips to mine? Yes. Was the opportunity to learn that feeling, to learn about the physical expression of my body, taken from me without consent? Yes.

I suppose the answer is no, that I've never been willingly, sweetly, gently coaxed into a kiss. I've never used a bodily action to demonstrate how I feel about a man. For five years, I've never remotely felt the urge.

But now, standing here with this incessant, nagging, devastatingly handsome nitwit it's all I can think about. As if my body isn't listening to the logic my brain is trying to scream at it. As if there is a force greater than me pulling me to the edge of a cliff, and I'm gladly following it straight over the edge.

"Pshh, of course, I have. Don't be daft." But my voice is too high, the notes of it too strung out and panicked.

Kingston rubs one large, olive-skinned hand over his

boyishly rugged features. "Oh my fuck, you haven't. How is that even possible? I mean ... look at you!"

I try to take one step back, but he follows, and the fridge is at my back. "I have *to* kissed someone."

"No, you haven't. You may think you're a brilliant liar, but you're actually pretty shite at it. It is a crime against humanity that no one's tasted those lips."

And now he's staring directly at said lips, and I can't help it when I run my top teeth along the bottom one. Kingston tracks the movement, and the familiar tingle he keeps inciting low in my belly bursts to life.

"Let me do the honor?" His voice is the deepest octave, a gravelly hoarse laced through it.

It's not a direct question, but he is asking permission. It's more than any man has done in my life, and I'm so jumbled with sexual energy and electric heat that I do the one thing I wasn't sure my body would ever allow.

I nod my head, inviting the man I've been holding at an arm's length to dip his mouth to mine.

I'm not sure what's come over me ... this must be the fever that Kingston Phillips ignites in women. One second, I want to throttle him, and the next, he's in my space, making my head swim with lust. Or maybe it's just time. Maybe I'm finally allowing myself not to feel guilty every time attraction settles in my bones. Perhaps enough time has passed that I don't see *his* face each time I think about being with a man. Is this my mind's way of finally dealing with the trauma?

That large body looms over mine, and I hate that he was right about checking off one box of my must-haves list when it comes to finding a man. I'm a tall woman at five foot eleven, and Kingston has another five or six inches on me. Why is that so arousing?

It's almost as if he's smirking at me as he closes in, the countdown to his imminent kiss ticking off in the back of my brain. My hands shake and the organ in my chest, the one I thought had shriveled and died long ago, is beating so hard I almost want to cry with relief.

And though I thought my brain would be in overdrive, tricking itself into thinking I was going to be attacked …

It's blissfully numb. There is a warm, fuzzy white noise drifting through my head, and the instant Kingston's lips find mine, my eyes flutter closed and thought itself ceases to exist.

There is only *this*. The gentle, wet pressure of his mouth against mine. The churning, pleasant feeling low in my belly. It's as if Kingston is stoking some fire I didn't realize lay dormant inside me. With every gasped breath between us, as his hands come up to frame my face, when his tongue breaches the seam of my mouth and touches my own …

He's wiping away all the rot and scorched earth left behind here.

He's making me clean. Whole.

The man kisses me as if I'm his dying breath and he's chasing it, and I have to wonder, *is it always like this?* Does kissing make you feel like you're both sick to your stomach and flying through the air at the same time?

At some point, Kingston pulls back, and I'm caught in the laser beam of his electric green gaze.

"Let's go to the bedroom."

That douses any budding hope or curiosity I had about exploring the tingles sparking in my flesh. Immediately, dread drenches me in its icy blanket.

I'm only the ripe old age of twenty, and I'm certain Kingston doesn't have more than a year or two on me. We're playing pretend, just children forced to grow up too early. We've placed ourselves into the adult world with our posh, expensive flats and fast times on the nightlife scene … and expect that to be enough to prove to outsiders that we're wise enough to direct the traffic of our own lives. It's all a sham, though. We're too young, too inexperienced, to act as though we've got it all figured out.

It's really that easy for him, isn't it? A woman lays her trust in his hands, and it's supposed to move at the speed of light. That's what's wrong with this life, with our fragile, young hearts. Everything moves too fast in our world, and at some point, we're going to come crashing out of orbit.

I can tell he has nothing figured out. And I may throw up the shield, causing everyone to think I do ... in reality, though, I'm just as lost as the man combing his fingers through my hair.

He's everything I swore to myself I wouldn't desire. A man like the one who stole everything from me. A man like my father; a cheater and a charmer, using his strengths to manipulate women.

"I ... I, stop. I can't do this." My hand pushes at his pec until he steps back.

His eyes are glazed over, an almost drunk state of arousal swamping his mind. It would be bloody enticing if I wasn't terrified of him learning two even larger secrets than the one he'd already rectified.

I've never been kissed. Well ... until ten seconds ago.

I am a virgin. Which, if that fact got out, would put another microscope on my already diminished sense of privacy.

Then, there was the worst truth of them all.

When I was fifteen, a man four times my age stole my innocence from me.

And to this day, I've never told another soul.

11

KINGSTON

We're by far the greatest team, the world has ever seen!
And it's Rogue Football Club, Rogue FC!
We're by far the greatest team, the world has ever seen!
And it's Rogue Football Club, Rogue FC!

The fans shout out our team song; the stands ringing out in melodic unison and raining their voices down onto the field.

It's more of a pump up than Muse or Jay-Z could ever be, and as I do a couple of high-knee sprints up and down the sidelines, I let the adrenaline of their joy wash over me. It may be the seventy-fifth minute, and our fans may already be celebrating an almost sured-up four to one victory, but I'm finally being subbed in.

After two solid months of riding the bench, Niles Harrington has finally called my kit number and told me to warm up. Now, the whistle is blown, and Alexander jogs off the pitch, holding up his hand for me to high five. I do, so, he slaps my arse on the way past and says, "Go get 'em, mate."

From the minute I step out onto the pitch, everything just clicks on. It's one of those matches that I can feel my body thrumming with competitive energy, and the need to home it in on one cathartic gesture. I've not felt it often enough these days ... but I just know, from the minute my cleats touch grass; I'm going to score a goal today.

That's saying a lot, and some may even call me arrogant for voicing it. But it's a gut check and an intangible fact. In my position, I don't score goals often ... but I just feel it today.

We're playing Mandem United, also known as the top team in the league. They're three points ahead of us in the standings, and if we can pull out this win today, we'll be tied for first. Of course, it's already in the bag. Jude and my other squad mates have ensured that. There is little to no chance that Mandem will score three goals in the next ten minutes, plus stoppage time. Though I guess in the game of football, you should never underestimate an opponent.

That probably goes for the game of life as well.

But just to make sure, I'm going to put my all into this small stretch of match play I get to show my coaches. And not just the coaches. This is my opportunity to show everyone—the trainers, my teammates, Jude, and especially my parents sitting in a luxury box ten rows up—that I'm bloody good at this sport. That I can compete with the best, that I've got what it takes to earn a full-time spot on this squad.

Maybe this is me wising up. Or maybe I'm just bored and welcoming a challenge.

Jude is up front, dribbling past a defender as he sprints away from me where I stand on the back line, between the keeper and the midfielder. I'm the last line of defense before our keeper takes all the weight on his shoulders. Though by the look of things today, Remus hasn't had much to stress about.

A complete wanker on the opposing team trips Jude, sending him skidding into the pitch. We all throw our hands up, and Jude milks the injury a bit as we're taught to do. But I can tell he's in genuine pain too, he's got to be smarting after that one. The referee claims he didn't see it and urges us harshly to play on.

That only gives the Mandem side ample opportunity to pass up the pitch, and quickly. Soon enough, they're in our zone, and I'm like a fighter pilot, homed in on which player has the ball. This is where I shine; I'm a pit bull off its leash, ready to do damage.

I see my opening pretty quickly, when a short vertical pass leaves one of their best forwards alone, almost cornered in by me. I go in hard, almost slicing his shin open with my cleat but narrowly missing it and gaining control of the ball instead. Inside, I'm beaming, sprinting with the ball at my feet. I bump it with my boot every few feet or so, just to keep the momentum going.

And my side seems to be letting me run with it. Luigi blocks another player and Jude screams as I pass him.

"Go for the goal, King!"

He's letting me take this one. I swerve around defenders, and at one point I almost lose possession of the ball, but then I'm back, marching straight to the goal like a one-man destroying crew. Their keeper's eyes shift back and forth as I idle with the ball, wondering how I should make my move.

And then I see him lean, a little to the left, and I know he won't be able to swing his body's momentum back in time. So I lob the ball right, skying it just enough that it'll go over the keeper's head if he's able to maneuver back over to the right side of the net. The force of my leg kicking its hardest into the leather.

The noise in my ears is deafening, and I can hear Niles yelling on the sidelines. It only takes a split-second before I watch the ball sink into the back of the goal, gently nestling and stretching the netting before rolling down onto the pitch.

"YES! *Yessssss*. Hoorah!" I throw my arms up in victory, pumping them as if I'm supporting the earth on my palms.

Sprinting to the far side of the field, I whip my kit off in front of the RFC supporter's section and beat my chest. The fans are going mental, cheering my name and rocking the seats so hard it sounds like an avalanche. Holding my jersey in one hand, I twirl it above my head like helicopter blades, joining the fans in their shite talking and celebration.

Suddenly, I'm tackled from behind, and I hear Jude screaming in my ear.

"You bloody did it, mate! Hoorah!" He's clapping me on the back, hugging me as my face is pushed farther into the dirt and pitch when our other teammates pile on top of us.

The entire scene is one of mass hysteria, and soon the referees are pulling us apart. They kick me off the pitch for pulling my kit off, of course. It's a violation, and I'm lucky I don't receive a yellow card for it. But by this point, my goal didn't mean much to the bottom line score, and we're almost in stoppage time.

As I jog back to the bench, Niles Harrington stops me with that hawk-eye gaze of his.

"Nice footwork out there, Phillips. You require more self-discipline, but it seems you've shown us just what you're capable of today. Keep it up."

I don't respond; he doesn't want me to anyway, but a small smile graces my lips as I head for the padded seat and plop down. A bunch of the trainers and other players congratulate me.

All I can think is that this is the feeling I play for. This invincibility running through my veins ... that's what makes this worth it.

Perhaps I should start giving a shite, because it's a bloody good feeling.

12

KINGSTON

fter hitting the showers, and taking a celebratory swig from the flask of gin Luigi keeps in his locker, I head for the player's exit.

Only to find my parents standing there, their faces scrunched in disappointment.

Instantly, my heart plummets. Most children probably can't wait to see their folks after a match like the one I'd just played, and yet ...

In the back of my mind, I was waiting for the criticism. Knew it was coming. And with nothing but my two-piece suit to protect me, I march forth for my sentencing.

"So, what is it this time?" I don't even bother to say hello.

Honestly, I'm not sure why they even attend my matches anymore. They don't seem to delight in watching me play, nor do they really seem to want to give up their respective schedules to be here. Whenever I encounter them in the stadium, Edward and Lotta Phillips just look extremely miffed.

"Your goal was very nice, Kingston." My mum steps forward, giving me a hug and a kiss without ever actually touching me.

"Thanks," I mumble, just ready to get this over with.

I'm exhausted from coming off the adrenaline high, and I'd rather not stand here and argue. It's no use. I'll take their verbal lashing and get on with my life.

"Your footwork was sloppy. You play defense, leave the goal scoring to Jude or the other forwards. This is your problem, Kingston, you're impulsive! Your attention span is that of a gnat, and while you could be excelling at your position and honing your skills, you instead chase the thing that sparkles in that moment." He shakes his head like I'm the biggest twit in the world.

"Dad, I scored a bloody goal! What more do you want from me?" I throw my hands out in his direction, almost pleading with him.

"For you not to celebrate like a foul git! All of this pomp and circumstance. Clap it out with your fan section and get back to work! You look like a bloody American taking your jersey off, running around the field like you just got your dick sucked for the first time. Act like you've been here, Kingston. You carry the Phillips name!"

Nothing I do will ever be good enough for my father. I gave it my all out there, poured my heart and determination into the time I was given. I increased my team's lead, even if it wasn't the game winning goal, that's pretty damn impressive on a professional football pitch. Against those players? They're some of the best in the world, and I'm just starting out.

"Fuck this." I swat a hand at my parents and begin to walk away.

"Don't you take that tone with me." My father grabs my elbow, yanking me back toward him.

He used to take this tactic when I was a boy, before I went to live at the academy full time. The use of his hands, but never enough that it could be considered abuse. Just a push or a shove here and there, and never hard enough to leave marks.

Now, though? I tower over the man, who was a shriveling shell of the Goliath that was Edward Phillips. I raise up to my full height, looking down into his eyes, and I see him rethink his approach.

"Not here, please." My mum's voice is calm and measured.

Per usual, she's only worried about avoiding a scene in public. Her sweep things under the rug mentality hails from the passive Swedish genes ... ones I appeared to inherit none of.

"Not so tough now, huh, Pops?"

He's so angry, I'm surprised there aren't blood vessels popping in his eyes. "One more stunt like that, and I'll talk to Niles myself. Get you traded to some junior league in Norway. Your career will be over."

The threat is laughable. "And why would you go and do a thing like that? It would disgrace the Phillips name, not just my reputation. Nah, you're bluffing. Have a good night, Mummy and Daddy dearest."

The endearment I throw out sounds more like a curse than a loving nickname, and I stalk off before either of them can demean me even more.

I forgo the team celebration at some rave outside of Camden. The whole thing seems dingy, dangerous, and half-mental ... which is typically my favorite kind of night. But, I'm knackered, both physically and mentally, and for once decide to head home.

The streets of London are quiet after our Wednesday evening match, the supporters long gone and the tubes already shut down. Most of the city's occupants are snug in their beds, resting before another full day of the work-week tomorrow.

What must it be like to live a normal life like that? Part of me wanted to know; the side that loathed my every move being criticized. How easy must it be to not have to answer for anything, or constantly be judged? Of course, I know people with quote-unquote normal lives have those problems, but not on the scale I did.

But the other part of me? It craves the spotlight. I was born into it, and therefore, bathing in fame feels more normal to me than breathing. I couldn't imagine not having all eyes on me, even if it means I have to take the lumps.

My brain is constantly divided, warring with itself. Is that why I can never make a decision, or commit to anything? Or is that why, when I finally do set my sights on the thing I want, that I have to go full throttle or stop before I start?

Parents, coaches, even my friends ... they're all bloody fed up with it. But the secret is that I am, too.

Charlton House is quiet as I walk through the lobby, not even the night receptionist looks up as I cross to the bank of lifts. It's not until I'm walking to my door on the top floor that the thoughts in my mind change from those of woeful inaccuracy.

Flat 602's door taunts me, no noise coming from behind it. I wonder if she's home, or if she's galivanting in some other country.

My mind flashes to three days ago, when my mouth took hers, giving her the first kiss she's ever had in her life.

Never been kissed. Poppy bloody Raymond had never been kissed before my lips touched hers in the kitchen of her flat. Of the flat next door to mine. The whole thing boggles my mind so much, I feel mad. Like I'd woken up in a world that's upside down and someone is trying to tell me it's right side up.

So, if she'd never been kissed before that, it's safe to assume she's a virgin. Unless, of course, she's pulling some kind of Julia Roberts in *Pretty Woman* shite where she only shags and doesn't get intimate face-to-face.

And don't start picking at the fact that I know my *Pretty Woman* references. Vance tricked me into watching it once, said Richard Gere was a posh bloke in it and that there was prostitution. He had me at that. When I watched, and saw what the movie was really about, I'd ragged on him for days. But now it was an inside joke between him, Jude, and me and we watched it whenever it was on cable.

Do I want to kiss her again? Hell, yes. But am I a fool for doing it in the first place? Even bigger yes on that one.

Sure, I haven't heard from Poppy in three days, and she's the one who threw me out of her flat. But it doesn't mean she won't become clingy. Suppose we bump into each other in the lifts, or a club, or at an event. I'm the only man she's ever been with, and it was child's play at that.

A shiver runs down my spine thinking about what expectations she might hold, or if she's possibly waiting for me to call her. To court her. Is that her deal? Is that why she's so inexperienced?

If there is one thing I'm certain of, it's that I am not the bloke for the job.

My pursuit of Poppy may have started out as a spirited challenge, but it ends here. I am not equipped to handle the emotions of a virgin, much less some needy bird who wants romance and fairy tales.

Nah, I am going to cool it on my neighbor. It's time to let my Kingston flag fly once more.

13

POPPY

Lonely might as well be my middle name.

I'm often surrounded by rooms of people, by parties filled to the rafters with those trying to mingle. But I don't have a single person in my life that I can count on to be there when I really just need someone to sit in the same space as me. Even if it's in silence, I have no one who will just comfortably hold my hand through a difficult period I can't quite talk about.

So, it's no wonder that on my rare day off, I'm snuggled in bed around ten a.m. Honestly, I'm looking forward to a day alone, one with a lot of binge-watching and quiet reading time. After traveling from Paris to Morocco and then to Tokyo in the last two weeks, my entire being is so knackered, it's a wonder I won't spend this entire day staring off into space.

I decide to order a delicious breakfast up to my flat, from the Zagat-rated restaurant conveniently located right next door to Charlton House. Eugene, the daytime doorman, brings up the tray they delivered, with a fresh daisy accompanying it.

"Miss Raymond, it's just as lovely outside as you are."

The flower makes me smile. It's the little things that can

make the biggest impact. "Well, isn't this beautiful. Unfortunately, Eugene, I don't plan on stepping foot out of my bed save for food today."

"Ah, a duvet day, then?" The kind smile that stretches his face makes me believe in humanity again.

"That's right." Confirming I'm going to partake in the British version of playing hooky.

After bidding him a good day, I take the tray and get back in bed, snuggling down in all of my blankets and pillows. I really decided to splurge on breakfast. A warm chocolate croissant nestled in a bed of egg whites, cheese, and spinach. Greasy, glistening potatoes, rife with salt and pepper. And an extra-large, extra-sugary caramel latte in a steaming to-go cup.

I'm a model, which means I've been on a diet since I was fifteen. Yes, genetics help a lot ... I'm naturally thin and don't have to work quite as hard as the average bird to keep my figure. But I still need to have a certain look, which is unfortunately only attainable through muscle-shredding workouts and grilled chicken consumption.

It's my day off, though, and nothing I do today counts. Being lazy, pigging out, shrugging off phone calls about work—today, those things will happen without worry or care.

I plow through the eggs, after switching on the telly to a random episode of *Friends* on Netflix, and move on to the potatoes. All the while, sipping my latte and chuckling at Ross' antics. I've always thought Ross was the funniest.

It's not until I take the first bite of my chocolate croissant, which I saved for last since it was the naughtiest item of breakfast, that I hear the dull beat through the wall. At first, I'm not sure what it is, the steady thrumming that is making my headboard vibrate.

Pausing my episode and sitting up a little straighter, I strain to listen for what it might be. That's when I hear the lyrics.

The Lion Heart

They're muffled, but sure enough, there is DMX screaming about gutting someone or shooting up the block.

Splendid, my neighbor is clearly home and getting his gangster on. All I wanted was a peaceful day in bed, with Rachel and Joey and the rest of their mates, and Kingston Phillips has to go and spoil it.

How not surprising. Kingston Phillips, ruining a girl in bed.

On the other side of the wall, the music grows louder and more violent. It's switched to some Skrillex track that has been mashed up with a 50 Cent song and I'm growing more annoyed by the second. He's completely interrupting my duvet day, and he's not even trying. He's just that much of a bugger.

An idea sprouts, and suddenly, my chocolate croissant and Monica's dilemma about Chandler are long forgotten. My jet lag and exhausted bones are not tired in the least ... in fact, I'm recharged and jumping out of bed.

Running into my living room, I grab the wireless Bose speaker I got for free in some awards ceremony gift bag. Pairing it to my phone, I balance it on the thick wood of my headboard, speaker side facing the wall. Pushing the volume button until the beeping ceases, indicating it's at the highest level, I thumb through my phone for the perfect song.

And then, I let him have it.

Demi Lovato's "Sorry Not Sorry" comes on full blast, her rich, husky voice singing about how payback is a bad bitch. Funny, I think the same, Demi.

At first, I can't hear anything but the blasting music coming from my Bose speaker. I even stand up on my bed, wiggling my hips a bit as sweet revenge courses through my veins. Is it sad that this is the most fun I've had in months? Sticking it to Kingston Phillips gives me a buzz like no other ... and for the first time since I discovered he is my neighbor, I realize that there are so many more pranks I can pull.

Apparently, Kingston has pranks, too. And louder speakers.

Because another couple of seconds go by, and then Demi is drowned out by Big Sean's "I Don't Fuck With You." Is that wanker mocking the fact that he hasn't even tried to contact me since we kissed? I mean ... not that I want him to.

Except ... blimey, I can't stop thinking about it. I've spent days in denial, trying to convince myself that it's my first kiss and, of course, I am going to stew over it until I go mad. That's not it, though. I know it's not. Because it's not the feeling of the kiss, or my performance in it, that I'm worrying myself silly with.

No, the thing I keep picturing when I close my eyes is Kingston's mouth coming straight for mine. The possessive, raw stare that captured his expression right before he tilted my world on its axis. The way his hands came up to frame my face, and how his body brushed against mine, lighting me up like a circuit board. When I close my eyes and let my head hit the pillow, fantasies of him crawling up my mattress and laying that big, strong athlete's body over mine, commanding my pleasure points ... that's what I'm thinking about.

Which only irritates me more, hence my stomping out to the hall closet, where I stashed one of the three Amazon Echo's the company sent me as a promotional gift. Running for the bedroom, I plug it in hastily, set the thing up as Big Sean curses and raps at his ex, and then start a song on the in-home assistant system at the same time I press play for the Bose speaker.

Simultaneously, Taylor Swift begins to belt about bad blood, and the sound is doubly loud with both of the speakers booming through my bedroom wall and into his. I cackle, supremely happy with myself, and dance around as if I'm one of her friends in the music video. Actually, I've met most of them, and they're pretty nice, as standards go for the celebrity world.

My song thunders through my bedroom, and I might be trying to wind up Kingston, but I'm giving myself a headache.

I'm about to turn it off, to claim victory and snuggle back into bed with my croissant, when "Roman's Revenge" by Nicki Minaj and Eminem roars through the drywall.

I swear, I'm almost knocked clear back on my mattress his answering cry is so deafening. My lord, he must have stadium-standard speakers in there, with enough power to put on a show at the O2! Never one to surrender, I try to hold out, turning the volume to ear-shattering levels.

About thirty seconds go by, of us fighting it out for control of the air space, when I notice there is no more humming on the other side of the wall. Slowly, a smug, satisfied smile stretches the corners of my mouth up, and I'm folding my arms over my chest in smarmy celebration.

Until someone begins pounding on my front door. Jesus, it sounds like he might put his fist through it. Quickly, I jump off my bed and race to the banging.

"I believe I win, then," I gloat, swinging the door wide open so I can shove my music in Kingston's face.

"If you two don't keep it down, I'm going to have to call management."

A blush steals over my cheeks as my other neighbor, Mrs. Clemens, stands in front of my open door. She must have knocked on Kingston's as well, because he's standing in the hall, a sheepish grin on his face.

And ... nothing on his upper half. No, he's completely shirtless, wearing black football-style athletic shorts and black sneakers. Rivulets of sweat run down his abs, and I can't will my eyes to remain level. The view is just too good.

After the trauma I've been through, I rarely look at men with any kind of interest. So why is it that I've never been attracted to a man so desperately as I am to Kingston? It *has* to be him?

Mrs. Clemens lives in flat 601 and is the most prim and proper woman I've ever met. From what I could gather from one of the doormen, she is a widow who inherited millions from her husband's untimely death. She's lived at Charlton House for almost ten years and is somewhat of a modern-day Mrs. Havisham.

I've only seen her two times aside from this and am thoroughly embarrassed that Kingston got me to stoop down to such a low level. Music wars through the walls? What are we, twelve?

"I am so sorry, Mrs. Clemens—"

She cuts me off, her already wrinkled face shriveling in distaste. "I expect this of that bumbling idiot." She points at Kingston. "But I assumed you had more class than this. Though you do pose for money in your knickers, so ..."

The look she gives me is so scathing, I swear half my face melts off. It could have to do with the fact that I'm currently in almost nothing but said knickers that they pay me to pose in.

Mrs. Clemens doesn't even bother to address our noisiest neighbor before turning on her heel and marching to her flat, slamming the door.

"Nice pajamas." Kingston's gaze sweeps over my body, and I realize I should have considered a wardrobe change before answering the door.

My spaghetti strap teddy tank and silky matching shorts are, of course, a set from Boudoir; what kind of top model for the brand would I be if I didn't have every new design, for free, immediately messengered over to my flat when they were released? Some of the higher-ups at Boudoir are inane, but even I have to admit I love wearing their lingerie and sleepwear.

"I was having a duvet day, for your information. Before, that is, you ruined it."

He rolls his green eyes that have probably melted thousands of knickers. "Yes, because I'm the one who began blasting music into the wall instead of coming next door to ask me to turn it down. You know, like a sane person would."

The blush that has begun to subside comes back with a vengeance. Blimey, do I feel immature that Kingston is the one suggesting that I act like a grown-up.

"Oh, *whatever*." Can I just shut my mouth? I'm only proving his point with the most primary school answer *ever*.

"Come now, love, you can do better than that. I've seen you way cheekier. Guess that blush and your stammering means *I* won."

And with that, the scoundrel throws a smirk over his shoulder as he too walks back to his flat and shuts the door.

I'm left standing in the hallway, mouth hanging open like I'm some gobsmacked fish, wondering how I wound up being the most to blame for this little stunt.

14

KINGSTON

Nothing like parental disappointment to make you rebel even further down a dark path.

In the week after my father got on my case about my goal celebration in the Mandem match, I'm late to two strength sessions. And when I show up to an integral practice thirty minutes after I was supposed to be on the pitch, one of the trainers loops Niles Harrington in. The manager of RFC lit into me, and my arse is still smarting from the proverbial chewing out he gave me.

It's just too bad I don't care more. The hot and cold attitude, the years of abandonment and verbal abuse … it does shape a bloke to stop giving two fucks. My father has conditioned me to feel nothing about everything. If you don't reward for good behavior, and punish for bad behavior, but then cross the wires and start doling out random emotions for something your child thought they did right or wrong … it really cocks a guy up.

That's why there is not a drop of sweat on my brow when I walk into the RFC facilities forty minutes late on match day.

"What the bloody hell is wrong with you?" Jude is up in my face from the moment I open the locker room door.

"Who's got your knickers in a twist?" I throw him a casual smirk, ignoring the way his eyeballs are bugging out of his head.

He's not amused by my nonchalance and takes me roughly by the elbow, dragging me into the bank of toilets past the changing area.

"You do, you fucking wanker. I've been calling you for almost an hour!" London's sex symbol is growing more agitated by the minute.

"I was playing that old Drake album we love. You know the one with—"

"I swear to God, Kingston, if you don't stop talking, I'm going to beat you to a bloody pulp. This is serious. Niles is furious. Rumor is, he threw a chair at the wall up in his office when word of your tardiness reached him."

Ignoring him, I begin unbuttoning my shirt. I am late, so no sense in dragging it out with Jude chirping in my ear. "I'd pay to see that. Also, what's with the word tardy? It sounds so dirty—"

Suddenly, I'm pushed back, my body trying to balance and keep up. Jude caught me off guard, and I struggle as he pins me against the cement wall.

"Have you gone mental?" I spit at him, clawing at his arm as I wheeze.

I'm in good shape, but Jude is in better. He's diligent in his exercise routine, where I, like everything in life, rely on my natural talent and slack off.

"Listen to me. Right now. You are in grave danger of throwing your entire life away. And you can stand there and mouth off, give me those shite retorts and act as if nothing matters, but I know you better than that, Kingston. Your father is a prick, we both know this. It's time for you to wise up, ignore his antics, and live your life how you want it. And you might not think you love football innately, but I know you do. I've seen you play, I've seen how much you love the game when you think there is no audience. Wizen the bloody hell up. Or ... or I don't know if I can stand by and watch this much longer. While you're in your selfish little world, feeling pity for yourself and trying to mask it with pranks and clubs and alcohol, there are people you can fall back on who actually love you in a genuine way. I'm one of them. But I won't stay around for this. I won't watch you burn your kingdom."

My throat is tight with emotions and lack of oxygen when he finally lets up, sending me halfway down the floor in a heap of gasping reality.

"Phillips, Niles wants to see you in his office. Now." One of our assistant coaches sticks his head into the toilets.

Bugger. I'm about to get chewed out again.

My squad mates are already heading for the field to warm up when I walk back into the locker room and Alex gives me a somber look.

"Go get 'em, mates!" I give them a cheery send-off, even if there is no more amusement behind my tone.

Jude seems to have sucked it all out of me, and for the first time in months, I'm not as smug as I try to seem. See, it's easy to deny the gaping wound your lifestyle and upbringing leave when you can mask the pain with cheekiness and attention and self-medicating.

My slow walk to the manager's office feels like a death march. He may just cut me from the club this very second. Or it will be some psychological punishment ... I can't decide which is worse. I try to memorize the halls of the RFC stadium, knowing this could very well be my last time walking these hallowed floors.

"Get out of my stadium," Niles Harrington barks as soon as I walk into the room.

I may be on an arrogant shite kick, but I know when to keep my mouth shut. "Sir?"

"Get the fuck out of my building. You want to disrespect yourself? Your family? That doesn't make a bit of difference to me. But you start disrespecting this club? My authority? You're out on your arse. You'll be a healthy scratch tonight, and if you utter one word to the papers about why, I'll end you. From here on out, if you want to remain a player for this club, you'll eat, sleep and breathe my instruction. Is that clear?"

A part of me desperately wants to say "clear," but the bloke is so furious, I'm afraid he may slice my head off. Besides, with the way my gut just went into a tailspin, it would appear that this display of power from the manager has me genuinely worried. It only took the head of Rogue Football to bring my temper tantrum to an end.

Three hours later, I'm half a scotch bottle deep with two tarts in my lap at a trendy Piccadilly Circus nightclub.

The room is spinning, and the music blaring over the speakers seems to transmit through my ears and to my brain seconds slower than it is actually playing. I can barely feel my limbs, a sign that I am way over the limit it takes to get me good and plastered.

But I don't care. Today was shite. This year has been shite. And how better to treat a shite existence than getting wasted and falling into bed with two kit chasers who seem up for any naughty thing I might fancy?

Le Ches, this nightclub, has become somewhat infamous for its close-lipped policy and raunchy debauchery. So much so that it's become an international destination for the world's elite. If you can find a place where shenanigans, many of them illegal, are not only accepted but encouraged and not spilled to the tabloids ... that's the sort of place many celebrities and athletes desire to go.

As it is, I saw one of Hollywood's A-list actresses swallowing two tablets of ecstasy at the table next to mine, and there is a rather famous gourmet chef engaging in more than spit swapping with one of the dancers on the stage.

From the corner of my eye, I see Poppy enter. Well, not so much see. I feel it before my gaze lands on her, the shift that happens in the room. Almost every pair of eyes turns, the chatter dims a little; the men seem to lapse into a daze. That's the effect she has on the human population, stunning one room after another into complete silence. She's simply too beautiful to focus on anything else. Laying your stare upon Poppy is akin to seeing an eighth world wonder.

Tonight, it's as if the club lit up a spotlight upon her arrival and is beaming it directly at all of those slim, luscious curves. The woman is tall, and it's exaggerated by the low ceilings in this particular speakeasy-themed hotspot. She's wearing one of those old-time flapper dresses in a light blue sheen, which only serves to make those big, gorgeous eyes pop. She's practically spilling out of the bust, and I thank God for her Boudoir endorsement deal that supplies her with all of those enhancing undergarments.

I've wanted to wrap my fist in those silky, mile-long curls streaming down her back from the moment I met her, and tonight is no different. It's as if she knows how much her hair teases me.

Her eyes meet mine, and I can see the small amount of friendly challenge or suggestive hope in them. It's the kind of look that down low lovers exchange. Will we meet at the end of the night? Will we play this game?

We played games the other day, all right. The music war was too good to pass up, and then she had to walk into the hallway in that wispy lingerie and I almost had a bloody heart attack. It had taken me less than a minute to toss one out after I slammed the door to my apartment. For weeks, since I learned that gorgeous being lived right next door, she's been at the top of the spank bank.

But, as I've demonstrated in copious amounts tonight, I don't care about anything. Not my career, not what would happen if my parents cut me off, or how much deeper I could dig myself into this hole.

I especially don't care about her. Poppy Raymond, a spiteful virgin who wants to be chased but not to give anything in return. A cheeky brat that is the farthest thing from what I desire; an easy shag.

No, my attraction to her is purely carnal, and if she's not going to follow through on it, I shouldn't waste my time.

I was about to botch whatever we had going ... if it was even going.

Watch this.

15

POPPY

There is a reason I never come to Le Ches.

The place is mobbed when I walk in, the most glamorous of people lining the walls and spilling onto the multiple stages. The club is located about fifteen minutes from my flat, but I've avoided it until now. There are stories one hears about this place; sex on stage, VIP closed-door rooms where nothing is off the table, drugs floating around like candy … and apparently an S&M room where you can watch subs and doms interact in kink and foreplay.

I like a drunken night out as much as the next girl, especially since I have an image to upkeep. But this place? It brings all of my nightmares to life. I've never dabbled in the drug scene, no matter how many tabloid stories or fake social media ads plug what drug I'm using to stay skinny this week. Although I know that there is a rulebook for kink and domination, I have zero experience in regular sexual activity. I can't fathom how anyone would be excited about being hurt and tortured. And the whole aesthetic of this nightclub is to abandon thought and give yourself to the chaos and hedonism.

That couldn't be further outside of my comfort zone.

But when my agent mentioned that a bunch of the models from my latest Riare, the most well-known upscale makeup brand in the world and my biggest campaign paycheck to date, shoot were venturing to Les Ches tonight ... there was little I could do to avoid going as well. These brands want your face or body painted with their products, and then for you to go and show them off. Make other women envy you, drive sales using your face and unattainable artistry a makeup guru spent hours perfecting.

Tonight, it's mass hysteria in the basement lounge. The club is made up of multiple levels and multiple rooms in what used to be an old bank. The lowest level is a room larger than the open concept living room in my flat, completely encased in what used to be the secured vault of the financial institution. I enter through the enormous steel safe door, which sits ajar and appears like it might trap us all inside if there were an attack.

Looking to my right, I see swarms of half-naked slags dancing on tables in the level's signature waitress uniform: a pair of lace black panties and silky white chemise. The levels each have a different uniform, and the lower you go, the more scantily clad the servers get. The debauchery is as fast and hot as patrons want it, and I feel like an outsider the minute I step inside.

Technically, this is my crowd. They're the class of people I rub elbows with. But I like to think that their greed and selfishness hasn't completely obliterated my personality or qualities. I live a life of charm, but I will never forget where I come from.

As I look to my left, I spot him. A lot of eyes have turned our way—four international models all measuring above five ten are not likely to go unnoticed—in the short time we've infiltrated the lower level. But it only takes me an instant to scour through the prying gazes, past the hungry licks of lips and overt catcalls, to find Kingston's emerald stare in the middle of the madness.

He's in a black button-down, black jeans, and black combat boots ... and looks so virile and forbidden that my mouth starts to water. Again, I question what it is that makes me want to run into a burning building when it comes to this man.

But then, my eyes shift, and I'm acutely aware of the not one but *two* bimbos perched on his lap. Right now, they're pawing at each other, flirting and trying to catch his attention with some faux-lesbian act. I roll my eyes dramatically, so that he sees the motion, and Kingston's mouth quirks up into a cheeky smirk.

I haven't seen him since the music war escapades about five days ago. I was out of town for a short trip to Vienna and then holed up in my apartment, sleeping through the exhaustion of the long work hours and travel. I could hear my neighbors come and go outside my door, but didn't dare make a move to confront Kingston in the hall.

After all, we'd only seen each other before the battle of songs when he'd kissed me in my kitchen. And since then, he hadn't bothered to call, text, or slip love notes under my door. He clearly doesn't care about me, or maybe he'd satisfied his curiosity about me. I'm sure finding out that the supermodel you were chasing has never been kissed is a bit of a letdown. He'd gotten as far as was possible with me, and now he was on to the next conquest.

I can't lie and say I wasn't miffed. It always bugged me if and when I struck up a rapport with a man who showed his true colors only days later. Many of the males in my world were like that. Only after one thing, be it sex, money, or fame. Not many I interacted with could hold a bit of banter, had a good sense of humor, or could make the butterflies I thought were long dead ignite in my stomach. Unfortunately, Kingston Phillips could do all three. It's a shame that he is such a shallow wanker.

As if he could hear my thoughts, and wanted to further prove my point, Kingston tilts his head at me in challenge, and then promptly fuses his mouth to the bumbling, giggling blond slag seated on his right knee.

At least his tongue was halfway down her throat when my jaw fell open ... he couldn't see my shock or hurt and for that I am thankful. My model friends had long abandoned me for the bar or their most recent arm candy, and I stood rooted to the spot, lingering just inside the bank vault door.

The show they're putting on is so vulgar and sloppy that someone ought to slap some sense into the man. He's pulling her greedily, and it's a hot ball of envy and disgust knotting my stomach knowing that I kind of wish I were her.

I roll my shoulders back, allowing only one beat to pass where my mouth hangs open. To those around me, I'm now cool as a cucumber. Sneering with distaste at the obviousness of the bird mewling in his lap and using a steady hand to hike my miniature Chloé bag up onto my shoulder.

Inside, I'm shaking. With rage, regret, upset, and staggering sadness. The last one is the emotion winning out, a gash beginning to open wide in my chest. Kingston might as well be staking my heart with the pointed stem of that wench's knockoff heels, that's how severely I feel the pain. It's irrational and stupid, but I can't seem to get a handle on it.

In five years, I hadn't regarded a man with anything other than fearful indifference. After becoming a victim of sexual abuse, I didn't think it would be possible for me to feel anything but distrust for someone I might be attracted to. Kingston has blown that theory out of the water and completely smashed it to pieces. It was only a few stolen moments, of which I tried to convince myself I regretted ... but that wasn't true.

I enjoyed the frenemy relationship we had going on, and I could have seen it leading to something. But who am I kidding? This was Kingston Phillips. A scoundrel, a cheat, a *manwhore*.

He's no better than the man who took everything from me, or the father who had betrayed my entire family.

Kingston barely cares enough about his own life or his own future ... who am I kidding that he'd consider doing the right thing by mine?

I've barely been here five minutes, but I've seen enough. As I said, there were loads of reasons I hadn't come to Les Ches before.

Turning on my heel, I was already thinking about soaking my injured ego in a nice pot of tea and turning the American version of *The Office* on Netflix. When I reach the valet, I request my vehicle. He's a solid professional, as he hadn't parked it more than a few minutes ago but didn't object or let any surprise flicker on his face when he hopped to to go retrieve it.

It was just my luck I hadn't been seriously considering staying tonight. If I'd had some drinks, I'd simply have gotten a car home. But part of me must have suspected how uncomfortable I would be here, and so I'd driven my own truck for a speedy getaway.

Paparazzi bulbs flash as I duck into my jet-black Mercedes-Benz G Class, setting my purse on the other side of the seat and buckling in before pressing my finger into the push-start ignition. My baby roars to life, and I smirk once again at investing in my favorite vehicle I've ever had. Before I bought this beauty, I wasn't much of a driver. But sometimes, when I had the rare day off, I'd jump in my car and take long drives out of the city. I'd end up in random villages or rent a room in the country by myself, where barely anyone recognized me or knew my name. It was glorious.

I rub the knackered feeling from my eyes as I drive out of the madness of cameramen and find myself relaxing as I venture down dark backstreets.

Until I come to a traffic circle and the incessant beeping of a fellow driver has me turning my head.

In the lane next to me is a black stretch limo, one of those ones you'd imagine a bridal party using. But instead of a bride and groom celebrating with their closest friends or family, I see a rather familiar man climbing out of the sunroof, onto the top of the vehicle.

"What in the bloody hell ..." I say to no one but myself, beginning to roll down my window.

The driver of the limo must be heeding the man's bellowed instructions, which I can hear from here now that the outside air is wafting into my truck.

"Don't stop beeping until you get her attent—" Kingston breaks off when he spots me staring at him as if he's some rabid animal. "And there she is, mates! The gorgeous Poppy Raymond, driving her chariot home all by herself. What happened, it's going to turn into a pumpkin at midnight?"

At this point, Kingston has more than half of his body out of the sunroof, and is haphazardly sitting on top of the limo like it's some bench seat made for specifically this purpose. He's pissed, that much I know, and his face is ruddy in its anger.

"What is wrong with you? Get in the car!" I demand, watching as taxis, buses, and cars alike race through the roundabout both of our vehicles are set to enter.

"Nah, what's the fun in that? Live a little, Poppy!" He cackles wildly, and a sharp ache in my chest tells me he's about to do something extremely stupid.

Just as I think it, he pulls himself the rest of the way out, hoisting his long, lean body fully onto the roof as the limo driver begins to roll forward. The arsehole plants his feet on the top and then stands, and I feel like I might be sick in my own lap.

"Get inside the car!" I scream, my vocal cords straining with fury and desperation.

He salutes me, balancing his hands as if he's on a surfboard. One bump of a tire or swerve in a lane, and he'll go flying into the middle of A3213 and be decimated by an oncoming double decker.

Now, instead of annoyance at his game playing, after he's the one who just stuck his tongue down some kit chasers throat in front of me ... all I feel is sympathy and panic. I need to calm him down, make him see reason.

What in God's name is he playing at? "Kingston, I don't know what you're on, or how you're feeling, but please—"

"All I feel is *free*, love!" He beats his chest and then flings both arms out to the side as the limo begins to enter the roundabout.

Without hesitation, I stomp the gas pedal to the floor, knowing that if I don't follow him ...

Well, hell, this will end badly for anyone. My heart is in my throat as I swerve and cut off the other drivers around me, getting honked at left and right. I notice flashbulbs going off, and I can see Kingston stumbling as he continues to try to play this game of chicken.

To live or not to live ...

Sadly, I know just how he feels. It dawns on me, as I risk my own life speeding through the streets of London, that we're not so different after all.

It's ten minutes of pure fear and raw panic coursing through my veins as I follow his limo back to Charlton House. Halfway through he sits back down, legs dangling into the sunroof, which still doesn't do much to ease my worry.

As I slam my G-wagon into park in front of our building, I see him dismounting with a flourish of his hands. No one follows him, and I realize he acted alone ... this wasn't a dare or a prank.

It's a person in a very dark place to risk their own life for nothing but the thrill of it.

Yet, he wanted me to see this.

"You're a fucking lunatic! You could have killed yourself." I stomp up to him, finger pointed directly in his face.

Kingston has the bollocks to snidely laugh in my face. "Oh, calm down, love. Just having a spot of fun, is all."

"You might be able to fool everyone else with this reckless, cocky, party boy act, but don't think I don't see through all of it. You want to take risks with your own life, throw caution to the wind and taunt fate or the Grim Reaper or whoever else you're trying to challenge ... be my guest. But don't involve me in it! I'm through with this, you got it?"

My outburst leaves me shaking, and I blink back tears. I can't watch someone else go through it when I internalize how he feels every single day.

I don't bother to listen to his rebuttal or judge his expression. If Kingston doesn't care about what happens to him, then neither do I.

I'm officially done concerning myself with my beautiful, broken neighbor.

16

POPPY

"Absolutely not."

My voice is a heavy stone in a calm pool of water, and I see the ripples I've caused all over Claud's face.

"Poppy, sweetheart, this is a big job." He uses that singsong tone on me that I loathe. "And they've asked for you specifically. After he saw you at the United Kingdom Television Awards, he knew you'd be perfect to model the new line of coats for fall."

"What did I tell you about working with him? I will not do it." Every nerve in my body is going haywire, and I suddenly feel that if I tried to stand, the paths to my brain would get crossed and I'd end up in a heap on the floor.

"Love, this is silly—"

I cut Claud, my agent and manager for all intents and purposes, off. "I made it very clear. I would not and will not work with Nicolai DeCallen. *Ever.*"

It's the closest I've ever come to telling someone about what happened to me. About what Nicolai did to me. Claud has been my agent since I got into the game; he's the one who discovered me from the commercial and changed my entire life. Back then, he'd been a platinum-blond shark in a three-piece suit and wore a diamond pinky ring. He never took no for an answer, drank espresso as if it were water, and always allowed his dogs, two miniature poodles, to lounge in his office.

Today, he is much the same, though his gut has grown a little from the constant indulgent meals, and his hair has begun thinning on the sides. From then until now, I could always count on him to have my back. He's honest, which is saying a lot in this line of work, didn't beat around the bush, and actually gives me a say about my career. Claud is one of the few people I can count on in my life.

But Nicolai? We've never discussed it in length, and I know that he knew what happened, but would never push it. Not because he was respecting my boundaries. Oh no, we were far too into limelight territory to care about such trivial things.

No, Claud would never ask me why I'd outlawed working with Nicolai DeCallen because he would have to do something with my answer. If he didn't know about my assault, about how a man four times my age sexually abused a fifteen-year-old girl, then he wouldn't have to have his models stop working with the most renowned photographer in the business.

If Claud didn't know that I'd been drugged and held down against my will, he didn't have to report anything. He didn't have to get the media involved or be a witness in the next takedown of the Me Too movement.

And I don't want to be that girl. The sad, broken one who was molested and who has never allowed a man to touch her since that day. I didn't want to get up in front of press conferences or news broadcasts or rallies and relive my victimization.

So, we didn't talk about it. But Claud has just crossed a line, trying to convince me into this campaign.

"Poppy, people will talk if you turn this down." His tone is anxious, and I want to smack him.

I cross my arms over my chest, calling his bluff. "Let them. At least I won't be the one talking."

This shuts him right up, and I watch as a shaky, nervous hand skims over the fur of one of the dogs perched on his lap.

When he called me down here to discuss a new offer I'd been made, I hadn't wanted to come.

I've had two sleepless nights, thinking about Kingston Phillips trying to hurt himself, or worse, in the flat next door. Although I told him I was done, I couldn't stop picturing the way his defeated, almost lifeless, eyes held my gaze after I gave him my worst on the front steps of Charlton House.

But here I sit, in Claud's gold and black, gilded office with windows overlooking the Thames. Because it's my job. Because when you work with the top agent in the international modeling scene, and he calls you to his penthouse office suites in the middle of downtown London to discuss work that would pay a pretty pound, you go.

When Claud first told me about the job, I'd been secretly thrilled. Best not to look too eager, especially with my experience, but I've been trying to land a LeatHER campaign forever. They make chic, faux fur coats that are all the rage among the posh elite the last couple of years. I'd been beat out last year and was still a bit miffed. But now, the job was mine.

Then I heard Nicolai's name and knew it was all a scheme. My heart had dropped to my toes at the mention of him. He'd done this on purpose, to mess with me. To bring the memories hurdling to the surface of my brain, to rip open wounds I'd been trying desperately to sew and mend. Not only had the man taken my innocence, my sense of security, and my ability to love normally ... now he was back for more.

"I will tell them you're declining. I'll sight sickness or a family emergency. You do have your sister's shower coming up, right?"

A sigh of relief exhales from my lungs, but the emotion still burns in them. Even when he was frustrated with me, he still listened. I know how rare that is in an agent. "Thank you, Claud. Yes, you could use that."

"You may regret this, Poppy," he warns.

"I promise you, I won't."

With that, I leave his office, needing desperately to descend the twenty-three levels below my feet and breathe outside air.

Just as I'm about to hit the button for the lift, though, someone almost barrels into me.

"Aria?" I say, glancing at the mane of silk straight blond hair as it whooshes past me.

She turns, and as I was the first time I met her, I'm struck by just how attractive she is. Aria is beautiful in that pretty, petite way I'll never be. The breakout singer of the year, as all the papers in London call her, has that girl next door vibe that makes her both cute and gorgeous in a very hard to find combination. From what I hear from those around our shared agent's office, and on the celebrity scene, she's also a very nice, genuine person.

"Oh gosh, Poppy Raymond. Hi." She blushes, and I find it endearing.

I walk over to greet her, spontaneously deciding to give her a hug. Which is odd, because I rarely let others into my personal space. Perhaps, after hearing the news from Claud, I need someone to comfort me. And I'm allowing this almost stranger to be a stand in.

"Really, you don't have to use my last name every time you see me. Poppy is just fine." I try to copy her smile, but find the genuine expression odd on my lips.

How awkward can I be? I don't have many friends, much less girls who are friends. The women I hang out with claw each other's eyes out for a Birkin bag.

And although I feel a certain type of way about her boyfriend's best mate, I do know that Jude Davies has an upstanding reputation in our world. The one other time I met her, at a club the first time I ever met Kingston, I could tell that she wasn't one to filter herself or take on a fake persona … much like a lot of other people I dealt with.

"Poppy, then. How are you? Did you just come out of a meeting?" she asks, and it seems like a polite curiosity.

"Yes, just had to pop in to talk to Claud. How about you?"

"My manager, Violet, yes. There is talk of Coachella offering me a spot on one of the secondary stages this year, so, fingers crossed!" She points in the direction of her agent's office, one of the three with a door on the same wall as Claud's office.

"Wow, that's amazing! I hope you get it, they'd be daft not to give it to you." And it's true, I've listened to her album. She's really very talented.

Aria shrugs. "We'll see, I'm trying not to get my hopes up."

We lapse into an awkward silence, and I speak before I regret the idea.

"Are you busy now? I was, um …" Gosh, Poppy, just ask the woman. "I was thinking of walking around the corner. There is a pretty little cafe and I could use a cup of tea, I could buy you a cup to celebrate—"

"Absolutely!" Aria nods her head emphatically.

I kind of regret it the minute we take the lift down to the street and begin walking. I didn't think about how I'd actually have to converse with another person.

My hands sweat the entire walk to the cafe, and I begin to nervously twist the napkin in my lap when we sit down.

17

POPPY

"My gosh, that scone is brilliant," Aria mumbles, a few crumbs dotting her lip. "I can't believe I didn't know about this place sooner. I'd be scouring it every time I come to London."

I chuckle and take a bite of mine, too. Orange zest and white chocolate chips light up my taste buds, and I close my eyes, savoring the flavor.

"Yes, it's a gem. That's why I don't tell people about it. But now that you know the secret, don't let it slip." I wag my finger in her direction, and she pretends to zip her lips.

The cafe is just two blocks from Claud's office, on a surprisingly quiet side street in downtown London. You'd think this area would get a lot of foot traffic, since it houses two of the largest companies occupying the business district, but it's too far from the tube station and isn't frequented all that much. I love sitting at the little Parisian tables they have set up on the sidewalk, my dark lenses shielding my gaze, allowing for maximum people watching.

"Promise. Not even Jude. Lord, he'd eat this place out of

house and home." She laughs, and I envy how casually and lovingly she talks about her boyfriend.

"So you two don't live together, then?" I inquire, sipping a bit from my teacup.

Aria shakes her head. "No, my father and I have a flat in Harlow, about an hour outside the city. He's been in remission from cancer for about a year now, and I think the city would just be too much for him. So I commute back and forth, spending a chunk of my days with Jude. But when he's traveling for a game or needs quiet or rest, I'm typically with my father. It's nice since I grew up in Clavering and am a suburban girl at heart. I get a taste of both worlds."

That did sound nice, and it made me a little homesick. "I grew up in Wrexham, so I get it."

She blushes. "I ... know you grew up in Wrexham. I have to admit, I've followed you for a long time. When I was in secondary school, your face was all over the magazines we used to gossip over in our bedrooms after school."

I bury said face in my hands. "Oh gosh, how embarrassing. So many of those teen love articles ..."

"No, we loved them! It was such a mystery who Poppy Raymond was dating." Aria giggles as if she's remembering times with her friends, chatting about crushes.

"It shouldn't have been. The real stunner is that I never dated anyone. Still don't!" I chuckle, taking another bite of my scone.

She raises her eyebrows, interested. "Well, since we're becoming fast friends here, at least I think so ... do tell. Is there anyone special? Anyone who has caught your eye?"

I have to admit, the flutter of silly fun that runs through my chest is a welcome feeling. I've not done much girlfriend gossiping, or brunching, and ... I'm finding it not so bad.

"I like your company, too, even if you are terrible at subtly asking if I'm shagging anyone."

"So, there is shagging. Even better." She smirks.

My eyes shift, and I know I'm about to avoid the question. What would she think if she knew I've never shagged anyone? "Sadly, no. My bed is empty and my—love tank, shall we call it—is equally as desolate."

"That's a shame. If only you had a dishy, notorious neighbor to help you with that problem ..." Aria taps her chin, implying way too much with that gleam in her eye.

"Ah, so I see you've spoken to Kingston. The dreadful twit." My mood sours just saying his name.

She cracks up as the waitress comes to refill our tea. "I see your feelings toward Jude's best mate haven't changed much since the first time you met him."

Aria was there, in the nightclub where Kingston first chatted me up. She'd been wasted, but our introduction had been charming, as was this conversation.

"The man is a total scoundrel. A regular Casanova. All talk, and all women." I flick my hair over my shoulder, as if to demonstrate how unconcerned I am with him.

Nodding her head, she pops the last piece of scone in her mouth. "Yes, he's quite the jester. Loves the attention, the taunting. It's all part of his act."

"His act? As if! Kingston Phillips is nothing more than a randy swine." I stamp my foot on the ground to make my point even further.

Suddenly, her eyes transform. Where there was once a hint of joking and good-natured feminine chat, now appears confusion, sympathy and unease.

"Poppy, I think you may have the wrong idea about Kingston ..."

"Psst, don't worry. He's shown me his true colors."

"Listen, I probably shouldn't be saying this, but ... Kingston has not had an easy life." Aria's expression grows pained, and I know she's debating with herself over whether to share whatever she has to share.

I roll my eyes. "Oh, come on. He's Kingston Phillips. He practically grew up with the princes and princesses of Britain."

She shakes her head, those blond locks shining. "You might think that, and in some ways it's true. But I know hardship, believe me. I grew up in ... well, not the best of conditions or family units. I had it rough there for a while. But I would have taken my childhood over Kingston's any day. I grew up with a loving parent, in a home where we discussed challenges and told each other how much we care. Even if our shelter was small and dank and we went without for a lot of years ... my upbringing was light-years better than Kingston's."

The way she says this, so gravely and so assuredly, has me sitting up straighter. "How so?"

"Kingston, he ... he comes from parents who don't just expect success, they demand it. Being brilliant at football was never a choice for him, it was just pre-determined that he'd bring honor to his family by being the next athletic superstar. There wasn't much love, consoling or pride from what I can tell, not that he's explicitly told me that. But ... you can just tell, being around him. His need for attention, to find passion with any partner who is willing ... it's all textbook behavior for someone who grew up with very little tenderness or compassion. I can't imagine growing up with that kind of pressure on my shoulders. Did you know his father didn't talk to him for close to a year after he failed to be recruited onto the English first team for an international youth match when he and Jude were thirteen? A year ... his own father. And from what Jude says ... the silence is better than the alternative. Kingston has never outright told me this, but I've seen his father after games.

Watched him grab him, throw him up against a wall once. My mind won't allow itself to go further than that ... I'm not sure I could handle the truth. His mother isn't much better. She's aloof, couldn't care less about nurturing her son. It's ... just very sad. My heart bleeds for him every time he lands himself in the next pile of shite. Because I know why he does it. To get them to notice."

I know from Aria's tone that she isn't gossiping, but merely trying to paint me a picture of why Kingston is who he is. I, better than anyone, should know that what happens to a person shapes the core of who they are, how they act. I'm disappointed in myself for not giving Kingston the benefit of that doubt.

I won't lie that I had an inkling of just how brutal his life has been. A victim recognizes another victim ... I see it in his eyes. I just refused to feel empathy for him until Aria metaphorically smacked me in the face with the truth.

Kingston is ... just like me. Abused. Whether it be physically, verbally, emotionally ... it doesn't really matter. We're all equally shattered.

And as her words sink into my skin, the knowledge of his brokenness makes my heart weep for him, too.

We are the same.

18

KINGSTON

Niles Harrington may have deemed me a healthy scratch from the game on Wednesday, but by Saturday, he has no choice but to play me.

Luigi pulled his hamstring and the third backup, the bloke behind me on the bench, is shite and Niles knows it. It's an important match, one that could seriously affect our standings and a run at a trophy, and when I showed up on time to pre-match warm-ups, I was told by one of the assistant trainers that I'd be starting today.

The rush of being back on the pitch fills my bones, the onslaught of it amping me up to levels I'd forgotten about. This is the feeling I chased when I couldn't be here. The drinks, women, drugs ... they were all just a stand-in for the infatuation I have with standing in a bowl, surrounded by thousands, playing the game I love.

That's what I was going for the other night, when I climbed out onto the moving limo in the middle of traffic. If I could just feel something, *anything*, that hit me as deep as this game ...

Then maybe I wouldn't need it. Maybe I wouldn't have to please my parents or use this sport to win their love.

I picture Poppy's horrified face through her car window, how she'd screamed at me when I staggered up the stairs to the front doors of our building.

She's through with me, just like everyone else. Why does that smart so much? I tried to convince myself that her disappointment, her anger and upset ... that they mean nothing. But the look of sheer panic on her face as I pulled the stunt, and the way my heart sank when she stomped away from me, tells me we both care more than we are willing to admit.

We've only played about fifteen minutes of the match when the ball is lobbed into our zone, right at my feet and I make a snap decision to pass it back to Jude. My thinking is, if I can try to clear it rather than moving with it and risk the other team stealing it and taking a shot on goal, then that is the smarter play. I don't always use the first thought that pops into my head, contrary to popular belief.

Except I don't get that far, because one of the opposing team's forwards almost slams into me, trying to work his legs through mine and take the ball right out from under my feet. So I redirect, aiming at Alex as I sky the ball toward him. He uses the chest bump technique to stop its momentum and passes it off to Jude who goes running.

The wanker is still on me though, and I can tell he's trying to start shite. He gets so close to me, he's standing on one of my boots. I elbow him, just harshly enough that I feel it sink in between the cushion of his ribs.

"Fuck! That's a fucking foul!" He throws his hands up, attracting attention as Jude tries to steal the ball out from under another player's feet.

The match is still going on; the ball being passed back and forth, kicked further out by one of our players and then dribbled back into our territory by someone on the other squad.

The referee glances in our direction, sees how the prick is

practically rubbing up against me as if we were playing that ridiculous American sport, basketball.

"Hey, you two there! Cut it out! Play clean." His voice is a whip, and then he jogs off.

Which only gives the bastard I'm trying to defend against even more leeway. He turns and sharply chops his knee into the air, promptly connecting with a part of my thigh. Just a couple more inches, and he'd have nailed me straight in the bollocks.

I double over in pain, the stinging slap of his bone leaving a throbbing ache in my hamstring, and I wonder if he's pulled the muscle.

"You bloody tosser! What the fuck do you think you're doing!" I try to throw my hands up, but I'm in too much pain to straighten my body all the way up.

Remus comes out of the goal, signaling to the ref for a whistle. Our keeper is all up in the referee's face before he's even halfway to me.

"What the hell was that? Did you see him knee Phillips? Right in the groin! That should be an automatic red card! The ball was nowhere near them!"

The ref comes over, holding his hands up to calm us and trying to hear everyone as we shout our sides of the story at him.

"He was all over me, how could you not see that?" I yell.

"I didn't do anything!" The opposing player is wearing an all-innocence expression.

Remus throws his hands up. "That's codswallop, I saw the entire thing! Red card!"

"I can't call something I didn't see." The referee maintains his neutral tone.

The stadium is already in chaos, fans yelling and throwing things down onto the field. I can feel it, the adrenaline threatening to spill over and out of my veins. They can't hold much more, the fury raging in my chest is about to explode. Out of the corner of my eye, I see Jude jogging over to us, and he puts a hand on my shoulder, as if he can sense what I might be about to do.

"I didn't do nuffin', ref ... he elbowed me!" The prick has the nerve to say.

That's when I unleash. I've had enough of trying to color inside the lines when life keeps kicking me out of them, and this is just the final straw. What he did should merit a red card, and instead, I'm going to be blamed for it, I just know it. I have a reputation on the pitch as a bully, when really ... that's how my position should be played. But because I carry the stigma of a rough rouser, I'm going to be put under a microscope for the rest of the match?

Not if I have anything to bloody say about it.

Cocking my arm back, I wind up and let my fist fly. It's a daft move, one that will no doubt cost me a red card, a suspension and possibly even my career. But I can't take this anymore. And that wanker who kneed me is going to feel the full wrath of my issues.

I hit him with a one-two, swiftly to the face, and he's toppling to the ground before I can even pull my left hand back and complete the motion.

"You're done for now!" One of the opposing squad's players screams, trying to get to me before I can even survey the damage I've caused to the guy's face.

"Kingston, no! What have you done?" Jude yanks me back, his arms coming up under my armpits as if he's trying to put me in a sleeper hold.

Not that I'm resisting ... I'm simply letting him pull me back as the other team comes for me, an arrogant smirk on my face.

A fist comes flying at me, a blur of knuckles and red slamming hard into my vision. I stagger out of Jude's hold; the pain branching out from where the jackass just punched me in my temple, sending its web of agony splintering through my face, down my jaw, and into my neck.

"Red card!" The referee yanks the dreaded penalty square from his pocket, signaling the end of the match for me.

I don't even bother stopping on the sidelines to get my punishment from Niles. I know better than that.

What I need right now is an icepack and about three bottles of tequila to numb the pain running through me.

Only when I step into the locker room showers, completely naked and alone under the spray of the hot water, do I realize what I've done. The throbbing in my temple won't stop, and the pain from being sucker punched is almost rattling my brain with every inhale.

My physical injuries are nothing compared to the emotional ones, though.

Because I know I've just ruined my career, and any shot at carrying on my family legacy, in this sport. I just gave Niles and every naysayer who has doubted me from day one, exactly what they need to bury me.

19
POPPY

Every muscle in my body sings with pain, the steps it just took to get through the lobby to the lifts was a slow, tortured journey.

My trainer kicked my arse today. I'm prepping for a photo shoot with Branel, one of the most iconic women's suit companies in the world, and I need to be in top form. I've been doing two-a-days for the past week, adding a second afternoon workout on top of my already labor-intensive hour-and-a-half sweat session I partake in every morning.

But once I have those shots in my portfolio, and the check in my bank account, it will all be worth it.

After all, I only have a few years left to model at the paramount level I've reached. At most probably eight years, if I strictly adhere to the mandated diet and exercise required. There aren't many thirty-year-old models gracing the cover of *Sports Illustrated* ... no, the elite level I'm at is a young woman's game. That means a handful of years to book every runway show, magazine shoot, and product representation I possibly can. And to invest the money from all of them wisely.

Because after that, I'll have to find something else to do. In a few years, I'll be washed up. I've seen it happen, watched the legends' faces become lined no matter how much Botox they pump into it. Watched their bodies sag after having children, watched their walks alter on the runway when the arches of their feet no longer allowed them to wear heels. I've seen it and heard it all ... because this is not an industry that celebrates beauty in the ones they've deemed old. Youth is the hottest selling product in our market, and once it's left you, it's time to pack your bags and make room for the next pretty young thing.

Mind you, I'm not afraid of aging out. Part of me actually looks forward to it, the blissful years of retirement after modeling. Maybe I'll get into consulting, or I'll work with the younger generation ... if they look up to me by the time my radiance goes away.

No, I'm not afraid of the future ... I just know that I have to hustle hard while I've got it, and right now, I've got it. Better to push my body, my career, and my prospects to the limit before it's too late.

As the doors open, revealing the soft lighting of my top floor hallway, my eyes adjust to the one thing that's out of place.

Where there is usually a beautifully woven doormat in front of my flat door, one I bought from Restoration Hardware the moment I'd heard the news that I secured this flat, is now a smelly, snoozing, large pile of man.

"Dear heavens ..." I stop midstride, trying to figure out if Kingston is actually breathing as he slumps over against my front door.

He's clearly smashed ... but did he really assume this was his home?

As I walk closer, I see a key jammed in my lock, and the evil eye figurine that was given to me as a gift to hang on the frame of my front door is lying on the floor. Yes, the moron definitely thought my flat was his. I wonder how long he had been jiggling his key in the wrong lock before he gave up, sat down, and passed out. What's more ... I wonder if this is the first time?

"Kingston?" I try to rouse him, shaking his shoulder.

He snorts, rolling over and hiccupping, and I get a whiff of his breath. Not just that, but the rest of him reeks of alcohol. The man smells like a bloody pub toilet.

"Get off my doormat." I gently poke my shoe into his shin, but he doesn't move.

Blimey, all I want to do right now is get into my walk-in shower, with the waterfall showerhead and steam setting I paid extra for, and bask in the healing properties of the hot water.

"Kingston!" I raise my voice, kicking at him a little harder.

I guess I could be nicer about this, but he is the one who almost flung himself from a car roof the other night ... after making out with a slag in front of my face. On second thought, maybe I should land a swift blow to his balls ...

"What the hell?" He finally rouses, his eyes bloodshot as he struggles to straighten himself.

"You're drunk. And in my way. Get up," I demand, growing more agitated by the second.

I throw his keys down onto him, and I see him snatch them and shove them into his pocket. "Trying to break into my flat, love?"

My voice is as dry as the Sahara Desert. "Yes, I'm trying to break into your flat."

"I knew you wanted to shag me, always knew it. Now come down here and we can annoy Mrs. Clemens a little more." Kingston begins to thrust his hips from his sitting position, and I have to contain the groan that's threatening to bubble up out of my throat.

"Seriously, you're in my way. You can stay on this floor, but not while you're blocking my front door. So kindly move your wasted arse and I'll leave you to that splendid thrusting you seem to think you're so good at."

He rolls his eyes at me now, probably because I'm not playing along. He pushes up off the ground, but when it's time to stand, he lurches forward, nearly taking me down with him.

"Bloody hell, who turned off the gravity?" This makes Kingston giggle.

He is so drunk, he's laughing at his own bad jokes. And now I know I'm going to have to heave him off my doormat if I want to get past him.

"Come on." I bend down to where he's leaning on all fours, threading my arm under his and trying to support his shoulders as he stands.

"You're practically scrummy," he slurs, trying to tickle my earlobe with his tongue.

"Stop it." I swat at his face, which I now notice is sporting a black eye the size of Germany. "What happened to your face?"

Kingston grins. "I was shagging some bloke's girl and he came after me."

"Figures." I sigh, disgusted.

"Nah ... just wanted to see what you think of me, love. Which clearly, isn't very much. I got a red card for punching an opposing player. So he socked me back. Hurts like hell, it does."

He got a red card? I know what they are, but that they're not supposed to be a common occurrence in football. What did he do to receive one of those?

"What did you do?" My tone is full-on accusatory.

"It's always my fault, isn't it? Nothing is ever done to me, it's always something *I* did. As if I'm not capable of being decent, or choosing the right thing over the reactionary thing. You're just like the rest of them." Kingston huffs as I support the bulk of him.

Honestly, I'm surprised he can even think of the word reactionary right now with as pissed as he is. Before I know what's happening, I have my door unlocked and he's dragging me toward it, the mass of his muscled form not allowing me to turn him toward his flat.

"No, I only meant to deposit you on your doorstep—"

"It's okay, love, you can admit you want a good roll in the duvet with your dishy neighbor. No need to be coy, you've already got me in your flat." He chuckles as if we're sharing some inside joke.

I heavily consider the option of fishing for his keys in his pockets, but I think he might take it as a sign of me coming on to him. And the last thing I need is two hundred pounds of Kingston thinking I'm flirting with him while he's well past wasted. There is no way I can cart him to his door again ... it was a difficult task just getting him through my own doorway.

It seems daft to let him stay here, but I don't see that I have any better option. I'll just lock my bedroom door and then kick him out in the morning. We're neighbors anyway, this is ... practically the same thing?

"I've just got the call about half an hour ago. My manager, telling me that Rogue Football is loaning me out to a fourth-tier team. Fourth tier! Me, the offspring of two of the greatest football players in the known universe. My father is going to disown me for this one."

Kingston is prattling on, not even seeming to care if I'm listening, as I turn the lights I have on an automatic timer off. They only serve to light my way into the flat when I arrive home late, and I start going through my shutdown protocol. Bolt the locks on the door, turn off the lights, set the security system. I deposit my keys into the tray on the table by the door and place my trainers in the coat closet. I'm about to make my way to my bedroom thinking that Kingston has fallen asleep, when he speaks again.

"My life is over. Well ... it wasn't actually very good to begin with but now? I might as well crawl into a hole and die."

I'm transported back to the cafe with Aria, and the things she told me about Kingston's family. He isn't making much sense, and I only vaguely know that putting a player, who is healthy and playing well, on loan is a bad thing. It means he's done something irreversible, to be sent to a club so much lower than his obvious top tier playing abilities.

From what Aria told me, Kingston is right ... his father won't take kindly to this. I don't even know the man, but I know men like him. He lives vicariously through his child, yet when any perceived shame is brought upon the family name, he'll cast every stone of blame back onto Kingston. He's a coward, not prone to love but to narcissism.

It wouldn't kill me to extend a little kindness to someone going through an obviously tough time. So, instead of booting him, or scolding him for putting his trainers on my white velvet couch, I instead retrieve a blanket to cover him with.

His hand catches mine as I smooth the crushed pink fleece over him. "Why am I so fucked up?"

That sea green stare gazes up at me as if I have all the answers, and my heart splits in two. Funny, I'd like someone to answer the same question in regard to me.

It's the most vulnerable Kingston has ever been with me, and I don't want to cock this up ... even if he doesn't remember in the morning.

"I think we're all fucked up. It's just how we deal with it, how much of a brave face we can put on, that gets us through the day. You're just having one of those days where you can't hide all your botched parts."

His fingers trace over my arm, lighting a path of tiny tingles as he seems to try to memorize the feel of my skin.

"You have no botched up parts." It's a whisper.

I nod, transfixed. "I do. More than you know."

"If you let me, I can fix them." It's automatic, his response, and I know his words mean way more than just a sexual innuendo.

Could it be that he sees the same victim in my eyes that I see in his?

For a couple of seconds, neither of us breathes. I let his hand trail my flesh, up my arm as goose bumps follow, and over the thin straps of my workout tank top. He reaches my neck, and my eyes shutter closed. The only audible noise is his gentle groan as his digits reach my chin, and I lean into his touch. We sit this way—him lying on my couch beneath a blanket, me perched next to him, allowing him to touch me in a way I've not allowed anyone—for what feels like an eternity.

I can't chance it.

"Get some sleep, Kingston." I pull out of his grasp and quietly walk to my bedroom.

When I wake in the morning, he's gone.

20

KINGSTON

The locker room is something out of a child's league, and it isn't even outfitted with more than two showers.

"This is bollocks." I grunt to myself, flinging my bag into the locker I've been assigned.

I'm used to the Rogue Academy training facilities, where no expense has been spared. And don't even get me started on the RFC home team facilities; the locker room was equipped with soaking tubs, cryotherapy tanks, a full-time masseuse and a fully loaded buffet provided from a world-class chef.

I doubt the Nartanica Football Club facilities even have working loos.

Of course, the inevitable happened. Niles finally had his ammunition to send me packing after I received the red card, and he'd done just that. But in a way that was even more devious than I'd assumed he was capable of. Man, when you made that bloke mad …

Instead of selling my contract to another top-tier team, maybe in Germany or France, he instead kept me on the RFC books but put me out on loan. It was what football teams did if a junior player needed more experience but couldn't be started on the squad yet, or if an injured player was coming back from physical rehabilitation.

But to send one of your best players out on loan, who was completely healthy and could help win trophies, to a fourth league team in the middle of nowhere? That was just a slap in the face.

The Nartanica Football Club is located in a small metropolitan area near Cornwall, but far enough away from London so that I couldn't commute. And kilometers away from any real football fans; from what I was told, their games only brought in about ten percent of what the stadium could hold.

I'd guessed Siberia, and Harrington had sent me to Siberia.

I'm not even sure what I'm doing here, or why I agreed to come. Because I did have a choice. Sure, I could have quit. Up and said fuck you to football and gone on to figure something else out. Lord knows my father wanted me to go that route when he found out about this snafu. Better to not play the game at all than not be the best. I was putting shame on the Phillips family ... honestly, I wouldn't be surprised if he asked me to completely change my surname.

Inside, I am destroyed. Gutted. A pit of shame, anger, regret, and dismay.

Because when faced with the choice, as Niles had my head on the chopping block, of whether to take this position or say goodbye to this sport ... I realized that all I want to do is play football. I'd debated and agonized and drank myself silly over the years trying to find out what I really wanted out of life, and now I know.

And it's too bloody late.

"Where is the masseuse?" I ask one of the players who walks into the dingy locker room.

My shoulders need a good rubdown after the long, bumpy

ride here. And I had to drive myself since I needed a car in this godforsaken town.

He starts to laugh as if I've told the funniest joke in the entire world. "You're Phillips, right?"

The expression I wear must demonstrate how dumb that question was. Of course, these guys should know who I am.

"Yeah, right. All hail King Kingston. Whatever, mate. No one cares who you are, and don't expect to be given the red carpet treatment because you came from some prissy, top-tier club. Or because you're riding your father's coattails. We've all seen the papers. That won't fly with the guys here. I'm Donnie, by the way, welcome to Narta."

And with that, he walks out, pulling a jersey over his head and turning his back on me.

What the fuck? I didn't realize I'd be walking into a hornet's nest, but, apparently, these guys like me even less than the manager of RFC and my father combined. *Splendid*.

Undressing quickly and pulling on a uniform, I hustle to make it to my first practice at Narta on time. Clearly, I'm not a welcome guest, and to have any kind of shot of making it back to Rogue, I'm going to have to work my arse off.

"Ah, Mr. Phillips, thank you for joining us. Mates, this is Kingston, he comes to us from the famed Rogue Football Academy. He'll be playing left back, and I want you all to show him the ropes here. Righto, let's get to it."

James Bleaker addresses his squad, who hop to after he claps. I met the manager of Nartanica yesterday morning when I arrived in town, after I'd been shown to the long-term housing hotel that the team set new players up in. It's on par with a Holiday Inn, and I can't believe I've sunk from my Charlton House flat to a budget lodging accommodation with no premium channels.

Talk about being humbled.

But, Bleaker seems like an all right bloke, and the team seems to be pretty competitive in its league, so I guess I should give them my best. The goal is to show Niles how much I want this, strictly for myself. No more trying to impress my parents, or live up to my name. A switch flipped somewhere between my red card and the minute I drove into the Narta stadium; I'm going to live my life the way I want. And that means keeping football in it, without the pressure of my legacy.

"You're too close to the keeper," a midfielder calls back to me as we set up for passing drills.

I snort. "Yeah, okay, mate. I think I know how to play my position."

"If the right back can't hold off the forwards, which he won't be able to because Patricio is quite good, you'll be too far into the penalty box to fend him off."

This lad has no idea what he's talking about, but I'm not about to run my mouth. "Got it, uh ..."

"Finnegan. I've been in the fourth league for almost five years. Which is five years longer than you, superstar. Watch and learn."

My hands ball into fists, but I take a few steadying breaths before the drill starts. Action got me into this mess, maybe it is time to watch and learn.

It's clear who Patricio is, the guy is faster than even Jude and can handle the ball like no one I've seen. I wonder idly why his talent is being wasted down here in the fourth tier, but push it out of my mind when the ball moves into my practice squad's zone.

Finnegan fakes out the other midfielder, bypassing him in an attempt to bogart the ball from Patricio, but the latter is too fast. I get ready, my heart thumping with enthusiasm for this game. Even down here, slumming it, I'm excited to be out on the pitch.

I should have known all along that I, alone, loved this sport, regardless of what my parents meant to its history.

And Finnegan is right again, the right back falls easily to the speedy forward, and then it's just me as the last line of defense. I get up in his space, using every technical move I've been taught over the years at the number one football academy in the country, but it's no use. Finnegan was right, Patricio drove me back too far, and when he sinks one into the back of the net, I groan in defeat.

"Told you so." Finnegan smirks as we walk back to our lines, ready to repeat the drill.

"You don't have to say it like that."

"Oh, but he does," Donnie yells from behind me, and I realize that he's the team's keeper.

How did I not notice him standing in goal?

Well, probably because I haven't noticed a lot of things. I've been on autopilot for years, not listening to coaches or bothering to learn new methods of the game. I've been lax on studying game film or sizing up other players who were leading the international scoreboard. I hadn't been putting one-fifth of the effort I could into staying nimbler, stronger, or more mentally quick.

And my blissful ignorance didn't just apply to the sport. No, I'd been shucking responsibility in all areas of my life. I let Jude and Vance down time and again, and yet they still stuck by me. My friends were top notch, and I owed them apologies for how selfish I've been through the years. When Jude lost his parents, and again when he went through that rough patch with Aria ... I'd been busy getting pissed and flirting with kit chasers. Vance was most definitely going through something right now, I knew he was, but apparently, he didn't feel comfortable opening up to me. It is high time I call him up and drag it out of him.

My worst offense yet, though, is being a complete wanker to

Poppy. From the beginning, I've treated her like a piece of meat ... and really, every woman I've ever come in contact with. I've been a selfish, cocky, immature twit who thinks there is nothing more to a woman than her arse and tits.

Honestly, I probably would still be thinking that way if it wasn't for the moment on Poppy's couch that smacked me between the eyes like a double decker bus to the face. No one has ever spoken to me in such a tender way. No one has ever seen the rotten core of my soul, stared it in the eyes, and told me they fought the same demons. And I didn't even have the nerve to stay and face her in the morning.

After that, everything shifted. It was like the scenes of our acquaintance played on rewind in my head, and I cringed at every part. The first time we met, I propositioned her before I even heard her speak. The second and third times, I'd been arrogant and crude. The fact that I made out with a woman right in front of her ... it was shameful. I was a prick, a nasty bugger.

That wasn't even the worst thing I'd done that night ... the way I'd terrified her with the limo stunt ...

I owe her so many apologies. And then I need to see if she'll give me one last shot.

Because based on the moment, that deep, intimate beat, I was pretty sure we are much more similar than I ever realized.

21

KINGSTON

The London Eye is almost twenty years old, so why not throw a party for it?

I guess that was my Mum's thought, even though I knew it was just an excuse to host a swanky charity party for it at her house. It's just another rouse to be Mrs. Phillips, to show off our palace of a residence and gain more clout. Or to gloat about her and my father's status in the world. There is always an angle with my folks.

Of course, I'm here in my monkey suit, indulging them, so am I much better? I pull at the collar of the tuxedo my mother had hand-sewn for me from one of her designer friends, and I can't believe the price tag on this thing because it's itchy as hell.

The tent that's been set up right next to the Thames is not your traditional sort of tent. No, this one has a parquet ballroom floor under the guest's feet, chandeliers hanging from the delicate white fabric ceiling, appetizers that have been made by a three-star Michelin chef being passed around, and more amenities that make us all look like privileged, fat cat wankers.

You wouldn't think spending two weeks with the Nartanica Football Club could completely change a person, and I would have laughed in your face if you told me a year ago that this would be how I would feel. But ... it's true. Something about going out to the country, about losing it all and falling to the very bottom of the barrel ... it's eye-opening. You not only see people in a different light and listen to those you may not have before, but I now see myself in a different light.

I always wanted to know what it would be like not to live the opulent lifestyle I was born into, and I got my wish when Niles sent me down to tier four. No one cared that I'd come out with a silver spoon in my mouth, and if anything, my new squad mates resented me for it. That only made me want to work harder, to care more.

As I finally stopped trying to fake who I was, I'm finding who I actually am.

And apparently, it's not one of these people. I hang off to the side, watching the London Eye twirl round its base in the setting sunlight. Sipping on a coke, no Jack surprisingly, I'm satisfied with just being alone and observing the view of the river.

"Kingston, there is someone you need to say hi too." My mum interrupts my thoughts, trying to grab my elbow and usher me into the hobnobbing going on around the dance floor.

"That's all right, Mum. I'm going to stay here." My voice is firm.

"Kingston, do not embarrass me." Her voice is sharp, and it's about as much of a yell as you'll ever get out of my passive Swedish mother.

Still, I don't want to play their games tonight. "I came, all right? I'm here, I'm sober, I'm not misbehaving. Take that and be happy, okay? I'll get on for the ride, and then I'll disappear. You're always embarrassed by me anyway, so does it make a difference either way if I keep to myself or go schmooze?"

I've never actually spoken to one of my parents with smack-in-the-face logic and truth. It must take her by surprise, because she doesn't have quick enough reaction control and her mouth falls open. My mother backs up, blending in with her guests.

I guess she figures that not responding to what she'll inevitably deem an outburst is the best solution.

Ten minutes later, the event organizers begin herding everyone to form a queue, to disperse into the various cars on the London Eye for an exclusive nighttime ride.

That's when I spot her in the crowd.

To be honest, the only reason I actually came was to see Poppy. I'd asked one of my mother's assistants if she was on the guest list, and they confirmed that she'd responded with a will attend. Of course, I could always go back to our shared building and try to snag her attention there, but my plan is far more devious. I couldn't risk her bolting into her flat, so I'd schemed another option.

She's easy to spot, standing so elegant and willowy well above most of the other guests. I can only see the back of her, all of those chocolate brown curls pinned into a thick, silky bun at the nape of her beautiful neck.

She's wearing a white column dress, simple with the back cut out into minuscule straps that keep it in place. I want to run my hand down the length of her spine and make her shiver … but I keep those thoughts in check.

I have an apology to make first.

"Excuse me, please … just, can I squeeze through here?" I elbow and nudge until I'm just one person behind her in the line of guests trying to board their giant Ferris wheel cars.

It's essential I get in the same car as her, because that way … I'll have her trapped. She won't be able to escape me in a wheel hanging four hundred feet above the Thames.

The wheel attendant is about to rope that car off when he sees me, and he must know who I am and that my mother is throwing the event. Because when I flick my eyes to the button he's about to press to seal the doors shut, he lets me pass, allowing me into the car.

And I'm face-to-face with the woman who seems to invade all of my dreams.

"You look stunning." I open with this, hoping I sound sincere because I really do mean it.

"Thank you." She blushes, none of the usual venom she usually reserves for me in her tone.

Ducking her head, I notice a shy smirk grace her lips. She must be thinking about our last encounter, the one before I was put on loan. I repeat that scene over and over in my head so often, I've worn out the memory to a sentimental old photograph.

"You left for ... I'm sorry, I realize I don't know where you're playing these days?" Thank God she isn't annoyed enough to dismiss me out of the gate.

"Nartanica, up by Cornwall. It's a little country town, not much around. But I kind of fancy it." My smile follows, and I see Poppy narrow her eyes at me.

It's not in a mean way, but as if she's trying to pick apart something new she's just noticed in me.

"Yes, it agrees with you. You seem ... lighter? The last time I saw you, Kingston—"

I don't want her to start off what is supposed to be an amends by talking about one of the lowest points in my life.

The car rocks a bit, cutting her off as we and the twenty other people inside throw out a hand to steady ourselves. Poppy and I aren't near anything solid though, so I let my body go rigid, locking my legs to the spot, and reach for her.

She lands against me with a thud, our bodies lined up from shoulder to toe. Our eyes meet, flicking back and forth in the close proximity to capture everything lurking in the other's gaze. The cutout in the back of her dress has my hands landing firmly on naked flesh, and it's cashmere warm under my fingertips. Poppy gasps as I let my hand graze for only a minute, and then I begin.

"Poppy, I owe you an apology." My hand is on her lower back, and I feel her sweet breath fan across my lips.

Those cool, ocean blue eyes asses me. "Is that so?"

I duck my head, trying to muster up the courage to say the things I know I need to. But then I rethink, knowing it will be that much more sincere if I banish my nerves and look her in the eye.

"It is. From the minute I met you, I have been nothing but a swine. A conceited shite who only wanted one thing ... and I think we both know what that thing is. You're classy, professional, elegant ... the kind of woman who deserves respect, not a catcall. What I did with that girl at Les Ches, and after ... you should never forgive me. I was in a dark place, I still am. But ... I'm seeing the light. I hope that you know that I'm trying to be better. I'm still Kingston Phillips, but ... maybe I can be a version of myself that isn't so haughty or self-serving. When you found me outside your door ..."

"Kingston, you really don't have to do this." Poppy looks away, but I can tell from how she leans into me that she's just as invested in what I'm going to say as I am in saying it.

"No one has ever been so raw with me. Poppy ... I think maybe you see something in me that I never even knew was there. And ... I think maybe I see the same thing inside you."

Inside my chest, I practically feel my heart being stitched back together. I've done a one-eighty, and while I'm still trying to maneuver through the last few degrees, it's clear that I needed to hit rock bottom before I could resuscitate my life.

Before I could try to give in to the way my heart beats for this woman.

Her mouth opens and then closes, those plump lips I've been fantasizing about tasting again transfixing my gaze.

"Will you be in town for a little? Maybe we could ... do something normal to get to know one and other." Poppy says this as if she's trying to fully convince herself it's the right move.

But I won't hesitate if she's offering something up. "I go back to Nartanica tomorrow afternoon, but how about I cook you breakfast? All you have to do is walk next door."

We're still pressed up against each other, and she slants a scolding look at me. "If you think I'm going to come over for some morning delight over eggs and toast—"

"That's not what I'm playing at ... though I might as well tell you that, yes, it's my end goal. I just ... want to share a meal with you."

How odd, that phrase coming out of my mouth. I've never seriously pursued a woman; they typically just fall into my lap, bed, or otherwise and then leave when I tell them to the next morning. I'm trying to ... court Poppy, and it feels monumental. I'm nervous and more than a little cautious, but this chase also feels more fun. No wonder Jude fancies Aria so much if this is how the start of monogamy feels. My flesh prickles with the mere thought of all the sexual tension that will be flying as I try to woo her.

And woo her I will. I'll be the best bloody courter she's ever seen.

"If you really want to apologize, you'll keep me away from that man." Her voice is shaking as she says it, and I can feel her grip tighten on my arm as I glance across the car.

Wait, that man looks oddly familiar. A flash of a memory pops into my brain, of Poppy bolting at that television awards show ...

When she saw the same man standing within a couple feet of her.

He's a smarmy Italian type, wearing a scarf over his tuxedo even though it's almost June. His smile is a leer he directs at the women around him, and automatically, I shield her from him. Not that we have many places to retreat to, we're stuck in this car for the foreseeable future.

"Come on." I lace my fingers through hers and pull her to the farthest point away from him in the car we can possibly get. Thankfully, he doesn't seem to notice us, but I *do* notice that Poppy's breathing has become erratic, and her pulse is racing as I feel it against my palm.

"Who is that?" I question her, ducking my head to look in her eyes.

She shakes her head, sucking her cheeks in and failing to calm her erratic gasps for air. "No one."

"Poppy, don't lie to me," I say as gently as possible, but she's going bonkers right now, and it's clear this man is the reason.

"Kingston, please don't make me explain here. Please ..." Her voice is desperate.

"Okay, okay. Shh, squeeze my hands and try to calm down."

Those cerulean blue eyes fix onto mine, as if I'm her lifeline and if she only keeps staring at me, she won't be lost to the current pulling her under.

I rub slow circles into her palms with my thumbs, and I've never wanted to care for someone more than I do her at this moment.

"Slow your breathing. In and out. In and out ... good. Just look at me. Keep your eyes on me. I've got you."

22

POPPY

Kingston helps me off the London Eye, supporting me as my skin goes hot and cold from the mild panic attack I just had hundreds of feet in the air.

Before Nicolai can realize we're sharing the same space, Kingston whisks me off to a waiting car and helps load me inside. Once we're alone, the cool black leather of the seat pressing against my back, I finally let out my first steady breath of the last hour.

"He hurt you, didn't he?" Kingston's voice is a bullet to my chest, when I've just now gained control of my own heartbeat back.

I can't find the words to confirm it, so I just nod my head.

"That guy? You were ... with *him*?"

Blimey, he thinks that Nicolai hurt me in the emotional sense ... as in we were *dating*. The thought makes me want to hurl up the coconut shrimp I had at the cocktail hour under the tent.

My voice still evades me, so I shake my head, trying to tell him no.

I can feel his eyes on me, how much they search every muscle movement on my face.

"He ... *hurt you*, hurt you. As in ..."

The dishy specimen next to me, in that tuxedo that leaves nothing to the imagination in terms of how fit he is under the expensive material, trails off. I know he's trying to work through it in his head, trying to wrestle with the image of Nicolai hurting me and deny it to himself. Oh, how many times I've tried to convince myself that it didn't happen. But it's undeniable.

"Yes," I supply weakly, turning to look at him.

I can feel the tears pooling in the back of my eyes, and I never thought this would be the way I finally told someone about what happened to me. Then again, I hadn't planned on Kingston being here or receiving the apology that just tore me to shreds and exposed my heart fully to him. Never had I imagined I'd go into a full meltdown, or that he would be the one to pull me out of it.

But when I go to search for the words, I find I can't begin to tell him. "Can you ... I need time. Can you give me time? I've never told anyone about this ... this is the closest I've come to telling someone what he did to me."

Kingston audibly swallows, and I see the evil rage pulsing in his eyes. He wants to rip Nicolai's throat out. A lion ... that's what I've come to think of Kingston as. He might as well be a prince of England, the lion is a national symbol. Fiercely loyal to those who he deems worthy, and brute in his passion for what he wants to protect.

And now, he wants to protect me.

"Whenever you're ready." The words are clipped, and I know it's not in frustration with me. "But know, I will end him."

He's furious that he can't go after the man who hurt me without knowing exactly what he did.

I glance out the window, wondering for the first time since I was led by him to the car, just where we're going. I feel his hand twine around my own, and I nestle my fingers farther into the embrace of his, even as my eyes stay locked on the scenes passing by my window.

We sit in silence as the driver pulls up to an ornate wrought iron set of gates. He rolls down his window, supplying the security detail with a name, and they press the button to open the barriers and let us through.

I turn my attention to the windshield where I can see the property unfolding as we near it. The compound in front of us is made up of several sprawling white residences surrounded by gardens overflowing with rich flowers and tall grasses. It rivals Kensington Palace in size, and I'm so stunned by the sheer majesty of it that I'm rendered speechless for a moment.

"This is my parent's home. My ... childhood home," Kingston supplies.

All I can do is gape, marveling at the place Kingston calls his childhood home.

It's palatial, so grand in every aspect that I half expect someone to be stationed out front, instructing visitors that they're not to take pictures of the interior. The architecture is pure English, with whitewashed stone and stately columns, curving molding, and small statues sculpted into the eaves of the roof. Kingston's house is not a house at all ... its wings branching off of a manor that is something out of a dream.

"You grew up *here*?" I can't hide the astonishment in my voice.

I've been to palaces, mansions, and some of the biggest venues in the world. I know what wealth looks like, but this? It practically rivals one of the Windsor residences.

Kingston shrugs, trying to brush off my amazement, but I see the hard set of his eyes. Anyone who assumes he's the good-time bloke he tries to sell wouldn't notice it. Though we haven't fully talked about it, our demons are compatible. From what Aria has let slip, I know he was abused as a child. This place probably looks like a prison in his eyes. And I just put it on some pedestal. Could I be any more daft?

"It's not that big of a deal." His voice is stony and I see a tic in his jaw that both has me wanting to lick the spot and comfort him.

Lord, how can one man elicit so many emotions? It shouldn't be legal.

As we exit the car and enter the groups of charity guests that have been invited for an after-party soiree, I marvel at how ornate every detail of his childhood home is. Kingston walks a half step ahead of me, clearly trying to get somewhere that is out of the limelight of this show of wealth his parents are putting on. Honestly, I wouldn't have come to this if Kingston hadn't helped me to his car, but now that I'm here, I have the fiercest urge to follow him.

I'm not even thinking about the fact that Nicolai could be somewhere on this estate; the only thing I can focus on is soothing Kingston like he just did for me.

"You're right. Diddy's place is much nicer than this." I sniff, my nose in the air, covering up my mistake for both of us. "Did you spend much time here as a child?"

I can't help myself. In a sudden turn of events, because this evening has been anything but normal, I want to know as much as I can about Kingston. I swore to myself I'd stay away from him but now I find myself following him deeper and deeper down the rabbit hole. If I'm not careful, I'm going to fall too deep.

"As little time as I possibly could. I was recruited for the academy when I was seven, and I'd stay there through each holiday. That is, if the groundskeepers didn't kick me out or my mum was sent to fetch me and drag me home." The bitterness is anything but unmissable.

A pang in my heart echoes through the chambers of the organ, sorrow filling my chest for a little boy who felt he couldn't return home. No ... not that he felt he couldn't. That he didn't want to. Even now, with the state my relationship was in with my parents and sister, I always had a little hope spring up in my chest when I ventured home. Though my parents were having trouble, and I was furious with my father, that comforting peace of going back to where I grew up always warmed my limbs as my car pulled into town.

I can't imagine dreading going home. From the way Kingston's body language emits tension, disgust, and loathing I can tell he'd pay never to have to walk these halls again.

And not for the first time since the night he gave me my first kiss in my kitchen, it strikes me that there are loads more layers to this man than I ever assumed. He is not just the bumbling jester out to give everyone a laugh and a romp in the sack. Kingston Phillips is gutted too ...

Gutted just like me.

Kingston turns a corner and the noise and music from the party are far away now, the air almost completely silent. He's not trying to get rid of me, but he's so tense that he hasn't looked back to check on me until now. We're standing in what seems to be a library by the time he turns around, his jaw ticking and his eyes hard.

"Sorry. I just ... don't like to come here."

Before I can talk myself out of it, I cross the room, loop my arms around his neck, and press up on my toes to do the one thing I've been thinking about since he gave me my first one.

I kiss him.

It's the first time I've initiated contact with a man, and I'm shocked that my mind and body actually let me without some kind of mental block. Every other time I've even contemplated being close with someone, there is a brick wall in my brain—the one put there five years ago.

But with Kingston, I don't think at all. It's just like the first kiss we shared, my mind goes blank and all I run on is sensations. The touch of his mouth against my own. The sweep of his hand down the open back of my dress. The way his tongue curls past my lips with such finesse, I don't realize he's made the snogging more intimate, but heat starts to pool between my thighs.

After a day fraught with emotional baggage on each of our parts, this is the ultimate cathartic act. I'm glad I had the nerve to summon the courage and snog him, because it's the best decision I've made in a long time. I want to feel again, and I want Kingston to be the one who makes me do it. I want him to be the man who wipes away the painful memories and the shame of what happened to me.

I want to smooth his tension away, too, and I pull my mouth from his to plant wet, open-mouthed kisses down his cheeks and jaw. The place where it had been ticking when he walked into the house, where I could see his expression filled with the ghosts of this house.

I don't know what I'm doing, have never gone this far in my twenty years. Though, Kingston doesn't seem to notice, because he's groaning as if I'm the one putting him in pain. I know, from many of the romantic comedies I've binged, that that sound means I'm doing something right.

His hands move lower into my dress, skimming over my tailbone. They're callused and large, and when his fingertips brush against the top of my arse, I shudder.

Kingston's voice is deadly quiet. "Poppy, are you not wearing any knickers?"

A furious blush spreads over my chest and up to my cheeks, and I'm glad my face is buried in the crook of his neck because I would die if he could see my embarrassment.

"Well, the dress is white, and doesn't allow for lines …"

Kingston takes a step back, and the obvious bulge in his pants says I was definitely doing something right.

"Jesus Bloody Christ." He bites down on his fist, regarding me with the most intense stare I've ever received. I feel like he could ignite my skin into flames by just snapping his fingers. "I … you aren't ready for all the naughty, naughty things going through my brain. And I want to respect that. I want to go slow. So we should probably stop touching. Or I won't be able to control myself. As it is, I want to pick you up and throw you over my shoulder like a barbarian."

His dirty words make me flush from head to toe, and I can't help the smirk that lights up my face.

"While I most certainly want to find out what happens when you throw me over your shoulder, you're right. I'm not ready. Kingston … thank you. I never thought you'd be the one I was trying to do these things with but, I'm glad you're the one."

The phrase just slips out of my mouth, and I want to slap my hand over the daft opening. Gosh, that sounds so hopelessly romantic like I'm a schoolgirl with a crush.

But Kingston merely tries to calm his heavy breathing.

"You would not thank me if you knew the fantasies running through my brain right now."

23

KINGSTON

True to my word, I stand in front of the flat next door at eight a.m.

I dressed casually, in tapered Lululemon sweatpants and a matching T-shirt, Air Jordan's on my feet. When I told Poppy I wanted to have a breakfast date, I'd been thinking we'd stay in. She outlawed that almost immediately, but it didn't mean I couldn't wear the same outfit I would have if I'd cooked a full English breakfast for her in my flat.

I'd told her as much, just so she didn't feel overdressed. That's what Jude and Aria had told me to do, when I texted them last night to ask how to take a woman on a date after I dropped Poppy off at her door and gone alone through my own. My best mate and his girlfriend had been so excited, they FaceTimed me in a flurry of excitement, listing off every question and piece of advice between them.

Don't talk about myself too much.

Ask her about her childhood, and why she loves her job.

Don't brag about past hookups—apparently they had very little faith in my ability to tame my arrogance.

Do feel free to flirt and touch a little, but don't come on too strong.

Don't order a completely absurd dish that will require you to divert all attention to eating it. Jude specifically told me no crepes, too messy.

Do not, under any circumstances, order an alcoholic beverage. I tried to tell them it was a breakfast date, but again, they had little faith in me.

Pick up the bill.

Walk her home.

And for the love of all that is holy—Aria's words—leave her with a gentle, passionate goodbye kiss.

Because apparently, if a man did not kiss a woman at the end of a date, no matter how well it went, there would be little hope for a romantic future.

I let the experts on dating know that there would be no confusion about that. It was all I could do not to go over to her flat in the middle of the night and demand more snogging.

"Wow, I am stunned you're on time." Poppy smirks as she opens the door.

Her hair lays in a long braid that she's pulled over her shoulder, and unlike last night, her face is fresh and bare of makeup. She's taken my casual notice to heart, wearing leggings and a long, sleeveless tunic paired with slip-on sneakers. Something wriggles free in my chest, and I realize it's warmth—it's the same feeling I felt the first time I had a crush in primary school.

I like Poppy best like this, and knowing that I'm probably one of the only people who gets to see her so relaxed, it's making my head a little fuzzy.

"I told you I was taking you out for breakfast. You'll learn quickly I'm not one to go back on a promise."

Poppy cocks her head to the side. "Didn't you promise me you'd stay away from my flat?"

Waving my hand in the air, I usher her to the lifts and press the button to go down to the lobby. "Semantics, and I'm sure I never used the word promise. Either way, we're starting fresh."

"At the crack of dawn, no less. I have to say, this sunrise date is off to an impressive start." She raises her eyebrows at me, and we enter the lift when the doors open.

Even this early in the morning, I feel the crackle of electricity that moves between us like a live wire in the enclosed space. What is it about lifts that makes everyone randy? Is it the slight chance you could get stuck in there?

"Have you ever played that end of the world scenario game?" The thought pops into my head and out of my mouth before I can censor it.

Poppy is standing just inches from me, our pinkies nearly touching. "What do you mean?"

"Say you're in a room, or maybe a restaurant. And you think to yourself, what if the world ended right now, and we were sealed off from the rest of humanity. And then you start looking around, thinking about who you would shag. Who is the most attractive, or who looks like someone that might be a good ally. Have you ever played that game?"

There is a smile on her full lips. "I'll admit that I have."

"The thought just popped into my head about what would happen if we got stuck in this lift." I take a step toward her.

Poppy leans in, even though I'm not touching her. It's a flirty dance, and one I very much like playing.

"So, you're trying to tell me you'd shag me if the world ended right now? Not much of a compliment, now is it?"

"Even if we were in a room full of people, I'd pick you." I wink.

She chuckles, leaning back as the doors open and the lobby appears before us. "You're a smooth bugger I knew it from the start."

"I never said I couldn't be charming. Just watch me." I take her elbow, helping her out of our building.

We walk around the block side by side, and I restrain myself from reaching for her hand. Technically, this is our first date, and Aria and Jude instructed me not to get too handsy. Though ... we shared one of the steamiest snogging sessions I've ever had in my parent's library last night, so I'm not sure this is a typical situation.

There is a small, quiet cafe about five minutes from Charlton House, and at this time of morning on a Saturday, there is barely anyone out and about. The hostess shows us to a table, and we sit, taking a few moments to study the menu in silence. Our waitress comes over, setting down two glasses of sparkling water, and asks what we'd like to eat.

"I'll have egg whites with a side of bacon, and I'd like potatoes. But can you chop them up and bake them into a hash with some turkey bacon? And I'd like an avocado on the side, with a small amount of hot sauce. Then if you could bring some coffee and almond milk? Thank you."

She finishes ordering, folds her menu and hands it back to the waitress, who curtly nods and then turns to take my order.

I can't help looking at Poppy with wide eyes and a smirk. "I'll take the full English breakfast with a side of steak and eggs."

I'm a growing man, who burns thousands of calories a day, and I need my fuel. Now Poppy is the one looking at me like I've grown another head as our waitress makes off to put the order in.

"Are you carb loading for the next month or something? My heavens, that's enough food to feed an entire army." She picks up her water glass and takes a sip.

I drum my fingers on my knee. "And I'll eat every bite. Who's worse, you or me? I ordered enough food for the restaurant, but you just read the menu and treated it as your own personal cookbook."

She grins, nodding her head. "That's right. Someone once told me that it's basically an ingredients list, and if you want something and know they stock it, there is no reason they shouldn't make it for you."

That makes me crack up. "Gosh, you're so privileged."

"Says the guy whose palace I visited last night." Poppy rolls her eyes.

"That's not my palace. It's my parent's palace," I grumble, and her expression turns to pity.

She reaches across the table, patting my hand. "I apologize, it was an insensitive quip."

"I just don't like to be lumped in with their lot. Yes, I was born into that privilege, and a lot of my more negative attributes can be linked to it. I loathe that I'm viewed as a spoiled brat, and I bloody hate that upper-crust air my parents and their friends have about them. As if they're above everyone. Dealing with that kind of haughtiness … it's tainted me. I used to believe I walked on water. Funny how getting smacked down to the fourth tier has shown me that my shite stinks just as much as everyone else's. Sorry, that was rather disgusting."

Poppy waves me off. "Don't, it's fine. And it's true. I didn't grow up with a lot, we always had enough to eat and new clothes come school time, but my childhood was nothing compared to where I'm at now. I get it, most people in this world do believe that they're high and mighty, loads better than the lowly people who help to keep them where they are. By buying the products, watching the movies, buying tickets to the matches. We're just puppets in their show, really. But money makes people mental. I'm happy you wizened up to it."

I hadn't meant to get into such a deep conversation over breakfast, on our first date, but now that we are here, it feels good to be able to talk to someone about it. Although I know that Jude and Vance *know* the struggles I have with being a Phillips, we're blokes. We don't discuss feelings. It would be extremely difficult for me to open up to them.

But with Poppy I feel the floodgates open.

"Growing up in that house was … well, I don't want to say a nightmare. There are so many kids who go through horrible things, and it's not as if I was starving or wanting for anything. But my parents they had and still have expectations. It's a lot of pressure when you're the offspring of two of the world's most famous football players. It's been Rogue or bust since I began to walk. I'm pretty sure I kicked a ball before I could even stand on my own two feet. RFC is the best club in England, the place where my parents decided to settle and build their empire. So, anything less is failure. My father …"

I trail off, knowing I've gotten even more intimate than I ever planned to. The woman barely agreed to come here with me, and now I'm going to tell her about the emotional abuse I suffered at the hands of the man who raised me?

"Blimey, it is too early for this." I try to laugh it off, my words having more than one meaning.

Poppy laces her fingers through mine and begins to trace circles around my palm with her thumb, just like I did last night for her.

"I understand what you went through. More than you know."

In this moment, I know we're both thinking about her confession in the car last night. My blood has been boiling ever since, dulling to a simmer but still retaining that acrid, poisonous feeling. Whatever that bloke did to her, he's going to pay for it. But she sees *me*. We see each other.

"Why don't we lighten the mood?" she asks. "If the world ended right now, who in this cafe would you shag?"

That makes me laugh, even through the lump of emotion lodged in my throat. I look around, pretending to weigh my options.

"I'd still pick you, Poppy."

Her eyes melt into blue pools of lust, and I know it might be far off but I can't wait to make good on that promise.

24

KINGSTON

After shipping off to Siberia, also known as Nartanica, after my date with Poppy, I vow to myself that I'm going to keep my mouth shut and work my hardest.

Now that I know I want nothing more than to play for RFC, to fulfill my own dreams, the ultimate goal is to get back to the club who loaned me out. And the only way I'll do that is by keeping my nose clean and playing my arse off.

Narta plays two matches in the week I'm back, and we win both of them. I score two goals in the second match, and I hope that Niles is monitoring my progress, because it's one of the best showings I've had in the last year. It is the fourth tier, but I find it's actually more difficult down here. Scrappier, the players have more to lose. Or gain, I guess. Everyone down here wants to move up.

Jude isn't much help on the snooping front, because I asked him if he's heard any whispers about me at RFC. He's such a Goody-Two-shoes, always keeping his brain focused on his own work. No good that does me.

Meanwhile, I've been texting Poppy as much as both of our schedules allow. She's in Paris for four days, but we've been talking as much as we can. So far, I've learned that she likes to mix ketchup into her honey mustard on sandwiches, and secretly dislikes modeling lingerie—a fact for which I'm sad about but at least I have the pictures to stare at if she ever decides to stop. Poppy also wants to own a cottage in French wine country someday, watches the show *Friends* when there is nothing else on, and the first concert she ever went to was some religious singer I've never heard of but apparently makes millions.

At the end of our breakfast date, I didn't miss the most important part. I walked Poppy back up to her front door, the one right next to mine. I had to leave for Narta in just thirty minutes, but that didn't stop me from spending a good five minutes bringing my hands up to her face, walking her backward until her back gently pressed against her door, and kissing her senseless.

Bloody hell, I could spend hours just doing that. And I might have to. I've been driving myself mad over the past week and a half, trying to think about how slow I need to take things. The first time I kissed Poppy had been her first kiss which means she is most likely a virgin. I don't know, almost don't want to know, what that bastard had done to her, but I was sure she had no pleasant experience with sex, foreplay, or anything of the sort.

I have no idea how to treat a woman who is anything more than a kit chaser. The easier to get under my duvet, the better, that has always been my motto. It's a big enough feat that I am trying to be decent and court her. But knowing how to handle a virgin with a history of abuse … I don't know if I'm cut out for that. What if I say the wrong thing, or move too fast? What if Poppy doesn't feel good when I touch her? The fear has nothing to do with my needs, but I'm terrified that if I make one wrong move, I'll scar her even worse than she already might be.

My squad mates interrupt my thoughts, three or four of

them rising in their plain clothes after this evening's practice. We have a match in two days, so it was a later practice today, but at least it was cooler than the mid-afternoon heat waves we've been having. Seems summer has come early to Narta, and the locker room wreaks of sweat after every session.

"Let's go get a pint, yeah?" Donnie doesn't so much ask me as tell me and then walks off toward the player's exit.

Finnegan smirks and then begins to follow his mate. I get up too, not wanting to miss out on an invitation. Plus, there is nothing to do around here and I might as well relax with a pint or two than sit in my hotel room alone.

The pub is directly next to the Narta stadium, so we don't have to walk far. When we enter, it looks like the same patrons who have been sitting at the bar for fifty years have already drunk their fill of beer.

"What do you want? I'm buying the first round," Donnie says, not bothering to look at me.

The Narta squad is warming to me, but there are still those who have a bit of an ice cap on their shoulder. Donnie is one of them; I don't think he's convinced yet that I'm not just a lazy twit.

"I don't care. A beer? Whatever you're having." I've never been picky when it comes to alcohol, any old kind will do.

Someone grabs a table in the back, and I slide into one of the old wooden chairs. I'm used to pubs in London, which are quaint and made to feel like the owner's living room, but this is at the far end of that spectrum. In fact, I'm pretty sure this is actually someone's den, complete with family pictures hanging on the wall.

"So, this is where you blokes hang out?" I open the conversation with a casual question, hoping that maybe I can win some of their opinions of me tonight.

It's the first time in almost three weeks that I've been invited to the pub, and no one is openly despising me to my face so that's a good sign.

"Only pub in Nartanica," Finnegan explains, taking a large swig of beer as Donnie sets it down in front of him.

"And the only place to possibly meet a girl in this town." Patricio smirks, suave as the day is long.

"Looking for kit chasers, Phillips? You won't find many around here. Again, we don't measure up to your posh London taste buds," Donnie quips. "And if you go anywhere near a girl named Maggie, I'll kill you."

Okay, apparently Maggie is off-limits, not that it matters. Part of me really wants to taunt Donnie with some testing jab, but the other part of me really wants to brag about the woman I'd kill for.

"You don't have to worry about me. I have a girl back in London."

"That's not a girl. That's a woman. *The* woman." Patricio wiggles his eyebrows at me.

"How do you ..." I trail off, realizing that they're all staring at me.

Finnegan fesses up with a shrug. "They all know you're dating Poppy Raymond. I guess they become invisible when you have them around so much, but there are paparazzi pictures of you two all over the Internet."

"You would be dating the most famous lingerie model in the world." Donnie says it like it's a curse and rolls his eyes.

"Fuck, those tits ..." Patricio licks his lips.

One of the other blokes on the squad, whose name I keep forgetting, tosses his two cents in. "How many times did you toss one off to her pictures before you actually got to shag her?"

My teeth snap together, and the icy anger is coming off me in waves. "Watch it, mates. That's my woman. She's also kind and intelligent, puts up with my rubbish even less than you do. She's not just some model, Poppy has been running that business for near six years, and she's a successful career woman. You're bloody right she's out of this universe stunning, but that's mine to make observations about. The next bloke who mentions her in that context again ... I'll kill you."

Donnie claps a hand on my shoulder and smiles. "Nice to see you so passionate about something, Phillips. Especially a good bird. Didn't realize you were a whipped bloke, like me. Good to have you in the club."

Who knew the way to get into Donnie's good graces was to get a girlfriend? It makes me duck my head and smile, and the guys move on to discussing the potential group play scenarios for the World Cup next year.

"How is the distance going?" Finnegan leans over to me, lowering his voice.

I shrug, drinking my beer. "The whole dating thing is still pretty new for me, so it's not bad yet. We're both busy people by nature of our careers anyway, so I think it might be the same if I was back in London. Though maybe this is better. We text a lot, talk on the phone some nights. It forces you to communicate, to get to know something about a person without jumping right into bed. I've truthfully never done it before. So, it's been ... exciting? That makes me sound like a twit."

Finnegan laughs, shaking his head. "I get it, mate. It's not easy with my wife back in Ireland, and eventually, I'll have to go back. She's put up with this for two years, and we want a baby. So ... this is probably going to be my last season. You do what you have to for the person you love and make it work however you can."

Finnegan shrugs as if he couldn't care less that he soon won't play football professionally ever again. To me, that would feel like a bullet to the heart. And the gut. And my shins.

Blimey, how daft could I be to ever doubt that I love this

game? Just thinking about giving it up someday, not even in the near future, makes me nauseous.

"You're married?" I clear my throat after taking a large swig of my Carlsberg.

He nods, a smile lighting up his face. "Erin is my childhood girl. We met on the playground in primary school, and I've been a sucker for her ever since. She knew when she married me that I wasn't done trying to make it in football, but it hasn't turned out like I'd hoped. There are bigger things in life, and I love her desperately. Making Erin happy is my number one priority. Nothing else matters if she doesn't have the life I promised her."

Damn, that was admirable. If you'd asked me a few months back, I'd say Finnegan was a bloody sap. But now I knew what it felt like to have feelings like that for someone. Maybe not as strong as Finnegan, who has been with his wife for years, and definitely not ready for anything resembling marriage. But I understand now, that pull to want someone's happiness over your own. To want to be a better man for the woman you care about.

"That's ... blimey, that's tragically admirable. I wish you all the luck, mate." I raise my glass to his and clink them together.

"And same to you, mate. May we get home to our girls soon."

25

POPPY

"Okay, so this time I want just a small smile as your falling, and try to sniff the perfume bottle as you're doing it."

The photographer instructs me as I stand at the top of a small ladder, looking down toward the stack of mats below. I'm teetering on the small platform in a bright pink ball gown covered in hand-embroidered flowers. The dress probably retails for more than your average midsize car. I also have six-carat dangling diamond earrings, my hair is braided intricately around my head like some Swiss milkmaid, and the amount of makeup on my face is starting to weigh my eyes and cheeks down.

We've been at this for hours, trying to shoot the advertisements for the new perfume Riare is launching in a month. If anyone saw what really went into the three or four stunning photos that come out of eight hours of tough work they'd probably laugh. And then be surprised.

Modeling really is work, there is hours and hours of labor that goes into getting the perfect shot. From prep time in hair and makeup, to studying what the brand wants, to channeling the right look and pose for the product; it's not easy. And that's just the beforehand work. The actual process of the shoot is intense. For this perfume ad, I've fallen over twenty times onto the soft stunt mats below. Riare wants the perfect shot of me falling, midair, while smelling the perfume with a satisfied but coy expression on my face. The overall feel of the ad is supposed to make consumers want to *fall* in love with the scent.

"Got it. I was thinking I could float my arm out, make it look as if I'm almost a ballerina or something. It might give more depth to the shot?" I suggest.

The photographer I'm working with today is on the newer side, but she's good. And I appreciate a woman in the driver's seat. I just find that I have a wealth of experience to pull from, and good instincts about what might land us the best shot possible.

"Yeah, let's try that, too. Good thinking." She throws me a thumbs-up, and I poise myself on the edge. "And go!"

Slowly, I let my body lean into the fall, trying to control every facial and arm muscle. Your instinct when falling is to shoot your arms out, or cover your face. The natural response of your body is to protect itself, and I have to fight it the entire way down. I hit the mat hard, because no part of me was trying to slow down my momentum. Picking myself up, I shake off the blow and know I have to climb that ladder again.

"That was a great one, Poppy!" one of the graphic artists sitting behind a large Mac computer off to the side tells me excitedly.

I catch him out of the corner of my eye, and instantly, my heart beats double time. When I casually slipped into our phone call last night that he could stop by the shoot if he made it back to London in time, I didn't actually expect him to come.

Kingston stands in the shadows, a smirk on his face and a lustful look in his eyes. His sandy blond hair is tousled, like he'd been riding in a convertible with the top down, and he's casual in faded red cargo shorts and a white Henley shirt. The summer ensemble has all of his brawn on full display, and suddenly I'm nervous.

Doing my job, I never get nervous. I've been modeling for brands for six years, the butterflies ceased to exist long ago. But one look from Kingston Phillips and they're flapping so hard that I have to press a hand to my abdomen.

He drove back to London just to spend the day with me, and after communicating via texts, FaceTime, and phone calls the past week, I couldn't wait to see him. How far we'd come from that dingy lounge the first time I told him where he could stick his arrogance.

Twenty more minutes, and the photographer is calling wrap on the shoot. Everyone claps, happy that we did our jobs right and got what Riare wanted. I thank all the staff, who have been one of the best bunch I've worked with. Not only do I genuinely appreciate the help of the people who work behind the scenes, but I also want only the best things said about my professional attitude if anyone were to interview these people. Your reputation is all you have, and when someone talks about me, I want them to talk about how easy, kind, and dedicated my work ethic is.

Kingston takes that as his cue to approach me, and instead of his usual slow and cautious hug, he marches right to me and wraps his arms around my waist.

Then he kisses me in front of everyone. His lips are soft but the skin around them is pebbled with stubble, and the scratch of it makes a delicious tingle roll down my spine.

After a few seconds, he presses his forehead to mine. "Hi."

"Hi," I breathe, feeling utterly swept off my feet.

Kingston has always been up front and obnoxious in his actions, so why should his feelings toward me be any different?

Well, I guess because I thought they would be. Every fellow model I've listened to, book I've read, TV show I've watched, they all demonstrate that if you fancy a man, he'll be distant and aloof. He'll ignore you in public and only chase you behind closed doors. That if you want a commitment from him, the relationship will be complicated and your heart will break more times than not.

But with England's famous football son, I'm finding the exact opposite. Maybe it's the change in Kingston's demeanor, or because I'm demonstrating that I have faith in him, it's actually working in my favor. Perhaps he only needed someone to believe that he could be a good man to finally be one.

"You look beautiful." His eyes don't leave mine, and it's like we're the only two people in the room.

"I feel like minced meat; I've been falling all day."

"Well, if you need someone to catch you, I'll gladly fall on the sword for that job." Kingston winks, and I find I'm no longer annoyed by his overt flirting.

If anything, it's grown on me as an endearing quality.

"I thought we could go have a picnic. I know a quiet place in Hyde Park and I've got supplies." Kingston holds up a soft cooler bag, and now I'm curious as to what's inside.

"Can I have a peek before I agree?" I say, teasing him and trying to peer into the bag on his shoulder.

"Absolutely not. This is top secret, but I know you'll like it." He winks one beautiful green eye.

"Fine, but there better be a feast in there, because I haven't eaten in hours and I'm famished. Let me get out of this ballgown and then we can go."

"Or you could leave it on. I've always had this fantasy about ripping the back of a corset open and—"

I slap my hand over Kingston's mouth because the production employees are starting to watch us, and listen, and they definitely cannot be privy to what Kingston Phillips might want to do to me if he were to rip me out of this ball gown.

Half an hour later, we're nearing the entrance to Hyde Park in the middle of a weekday. As promised, he has the Uber drop of us at a desolate corner of the park, and winds onto a walking path that I know for a fact not many people venture onto. I used to rent a flat directly across the park and would take a morning run past the grounds that housed Wills and Kate.

Typically, two people in our professions could not just walk around Hyde Park without security, but Kingston seems to have accounted for this. He's wearing a hat slung low over his eyes and bought me a cute fedora that he handed me in the car. "Wear this." He'd smiled and helped me fix it low over my hair that I'd brushed out from the shoot. I was still wearing entirely too much makeup and had body glitter on my arms, but at least I'd ditched the giant frock back at the studio.

"All right, here's what we've got." Kingston settles onto the blanket he just spread on the grass and begins pulling things from the bag that was previously under lock and key on his shoulder.

Sinking down, I join him on the soft plaid, thinking about how normal this all feels. I don't get to do normal very often, and I'm sure Kingston doesn't either, so it means a lot that he's trying to create it for us.

"You did not ..." I grin as he hands me the cardboard sandwich box.

"Oh, I did. I had to see what all the rage was about. So I walked into a Tesco, neat place by the way, and selected the best of the best. I couldn't decide so I bought every two-pound meal deal sandwich available. The cashier thought I was mental though she recognized me toward the end and I signed an autograph so I think I redeemed myself."

"I can't believe you bought me a Tesco meal deal!" I'm practically giddy.

Surveying his purchases, I see my favorite, crawfish and mayonnaise. I grab that before he can claim it and add a bag of spicy Thai crisps to my pile. Then I survey the drinks he picked out, and finish my meal deal off with a strawberry lemonade.

"Well, you're very decisive." Kingston laughs, watching me shield all of my picks from him.

"I've seen you eat, I know how quick one has to be when your appetite is involved."

Kingston smiles a lopsided smirk that does dangerous things to my heart and gut. "Touché."

He grabs two sandwich containers, three bags of crisps, and a large water bottle, then starts tearing into all of it. I lean back on my elbows, slowly eating my sandwich and tilting my head back to let the sun wash down on my face.

"This is perfect. Thank you, Kingston." I glance at him, and his cheeks take on the tiniest hint of color.

I think he might have been watching me. "I wanted to do something nice for you. I ... I'm not used to having that urge."

"Well, I dare say you're very good at following through on the instinct." Lord is he adorable.

"Did you know that there are paparazzi pictures of us on the Internet? They're calling us Popston." He slants a sideways glance at me.

I can't help but snort. "It's not the worst celebrity couple name."

Kingston bites into a ham and cheese sandwich. "So, we're a couple?"

My hand stops midway to my mouth, and I lock eyes with him. Gulping, I didn't realize what I said until he posed the question like that.

"I don't know, are we?" My heart is beating so hard.

He sets his sandwich down and picks up one of my hands. His eyes seem to be searching for something in mine.

"I've never been in a relationship or part of a couple. But I want to try it ... with you."

Kingston doesn't add anything about if I want that, too. He's just stating what he wants, no second-guessing, no doubting.

"Neither have I. So, I guess we're going to be each other's firsts." I blush because my words mean more than just committing to another person in a monogamous relationship, and we both know it.

Before I can blink, Kingston launches himself at me, tackling me softly and covering my mouth with his. It takes me a minute to stop giggling, the fibers of the blanket tickling my neck while his beard tickles my lips. But when I do, I give in, letting him stoke the fire that begins ravaging my system, the heat of the flames licking up the back of my thighs and spine.

The pure pleasure of his weight over me, the sun shining down on us, the seclusion of this hidden nook in the park; I could lose myself in Kingston and never want to be found.

He pulls back slowly, a large, goofy grin on his face and promptly steals my breath.

Kingston's tone is husky when he says, "I hope the paparazzi took some good photographs of that. Maybe I'll make one my new Instagram profile picture."

26

KINGSTON

Surprisingly, life and my attitude toward it only turned around when I got demoted and loaned.

My love for football has returned full force, I'm actually working together with my squad, partying and getting pissed beyond all recognition has lost its shine, and for the first time in maybe ever, the dedication to being the right kind of man is flowing through my veins.

One of the best things about failing, in most people's eyes anyway, is that my parents couldn't care less about me now. In my position, that's a hundred times better than having them all over my arse to live up to their impossible standards of who I should be. My father hasn't bothered to talk to me in months, and that's just splendid. No pressure means I can play the game the way I want, train without someone breathing down my neck, and the three of us don't have to pretend that we love each other just because we're a family. If an outsider ever sat down at our rare, uncomfortable suppers, it would be apparent within the first seconds that my mother, father, and I are practically strangers.

My friends have always been my family, anyhow. Jude,

Vance, and I are a band of brothers and counted on each other growing up way more than anyone else in our lives. That's what happens when a sport is your lifeblood, and your parents ship you off at the age of seven in hopes of glory rather than the desire to raise you on their own. Their disappointment, and subsequent abandonment since I've been sent to Narta, should affect me more than it has, and it might be sad I'm not more upset, but I'm simply not.

But the most significant part of my one-eighty? Well, that's not a hard answer.

Poppy.

Who knew I had it in me? I'm someone's boyfriend. I am one half of a couple. There is a woman who can stand me long enough and thinks I'm charming rather than a smarmy sleaze bag, to let me care for her.

Of course, the other unfortunate part of falling for someone at the moment my life took a turn out of the regular is that I'm constantly away from her. Not that the distance is a horrid thing, it's forcing me to slow things down and really understand Poppy. We communicate so much that it's making me feel as if I know her and see her more than I do. I suppose this is the good stuff, the meat and potatoes of a relationship that people always claim makes it stronger.

"Hi," Poppy says into the phone, and I can tell she's on speaker.

"Hey, you." I smile to myself and feel like a total twit.

But, if I have to be a twit, at least I get to fancy Poppy while I do it.

"How was the film session?" she asks, and I can tell she's distracted.

I shrug as if she can see me. "It was okay, we went over some footwork that all the defensive players have to work on, and then

The Lion Heart

sized up the opposing team for next week. My neck is sore from the morning training session though."

"If I were there, I'd rub it for you." Her smooth voice caresses my ear and I'm instantly sporting a hard-on.

The other unfortunate thing about being far from Poppy most days of the week? We can't take our relationship to the next physical level. Having a glimpse into the underlying trauma left from her abuse, it's obvious we need to take things slowly. When we are together, the snogging is heavy and desperate, and I can breathe a little easier knowing she's comfortable and seems to welcome it.

"What are you doing right now?" I lean back on my pillows.

Wow, if that's not the line of lines. If Poppy were any wiser to the inner workings of a man's brain, she would know that I'm trying to initiate some mobile sexual activity.

My search history is a bunch of open windows about sexual abuse victims and how to respect their boundaries. One of the websites I got sucked into suggested having an open dialogue about sex, whether it was written, spoken, or communicated in person. Sometimes, it's easier for someone who has been through that kind of trauma to talk about physical contact before engaging in it. And the best thing my naughty but cautious brain could think of was helping her touch herself, with my voice detailing the very pleasurable things I'd do to her body when she was ready.

So, yes, I was trying to have phone sex with her and toss one off while she did ... but it was still mostly for her benefit.

"Trying to unclog the drain in my kitchen sink. It's all plugged up. I think the ginger from my sushi lunch is what's mucked it up." She sounds far off, and I can just imagine the independent woman she is refusing to call for help.

She's probably up to her elbows in the kitchen sink with

some sort of tool trying to fix it herself. The image makes me smile, something I do a lot when I think of Poppy.

"Well, there is something else that needs unclogging, and I think you could help me with it." Blimey, that's cheesy.

Her end of the phone is silent for a beat. When Poppy does speak, her voice is a mix of amusement and confusion. "Are you trying to seduce me over the phone?"

"That's exactly what I'm trying to do. Now, go into your bedroom, shut off the lights, light a candle and lie on the bed." My instructions are gentle, but I hope she doesn't give me pushback.

"Kingston, don't be cheeky."

Of course, she can't just do as she's told. "Poppy, I want to unwind with you, and this ... it could be a good step for us. Me here and you there."

I hope she understands what I'm trying to say, that I'm only trying to be delicate with her boundaries and making her more comfortable with me.

A sigh comes through the receiver, but I hear her moving. After a few seconds, her voice comes in clearer, meaning she's taken me off speaker phone. "Okay, I'm lying down on the bed."

My cock grows impossibly harder at the thought of her body sprawled on the sheets. "Good. Now, what are you wearing?"

I slip my hand inside the waistband of my shorts, past my boxers, until I grip my length in my fist.

"A black tank top and soft gray shorts," Poppy answers, and I can tell her breathing has changed.

"Do you have a bra on? What kind of panties?" My voice is husky as I stroke slowly, imagining her on the bed.

"No bra. Light pink lace boy shorts," she whispers, and I'm flooded with lust.

I can't help but stroke myself, even though I know I should slow it down. "I want you to touch yourself for me, love."

"Where?" she asks, but I hear the rustle of sheets and know she's squirming already.

"Spread your legs. Inch your hand past the waistband of your shorts, into your panties, and coat a finger in your wetness."

Bloody hell, I was going to make myself come before I even talked her through an orgasm.

"Oh my," she breathes, and I can just picture her eyes shuttering closed.

"How does that feel? I can imagine you making yourself feel good, using that finger to trace up and down your seam."

"Kingston ... yes ..."

She's fully into this, and my balls draw up, tensing with anticipation as I continue to jerk my shaft. The blood vessels in my cock expand, rigid and screaming with the need to release. It was rather easy to accomplish this, convincing her to go along with my lust-filled plans. I know in this moment that she needed this, needed the physical release that I could give her in the only way she could tolerate it right now.

"You're so bloody sexy. I'm jacking myself to the thought of you. I fantasize about your hair splayed across your pillows, your top riding up past your navel, the shape of your breasts jiggling in your top as you pleasure yourself. Those fingers just playing with your beautiful pussy; God, I can't wait to taste it."

Poppy lets out a desperate mewl on the other end, and I know she's getting close to climaxing. I'm right there with her, my short leash unusual save for the lack of sex in the past few months. Or the fact that I'm having phone sex with the most gorgeous creature my eyes have ever beheld.

"My cock is so hard for you, I'm stroking it faster now just thinking about how beautiful you're going to look when you come. Do you want to come for me, love?"

Her breathing is a rhythmic thrumming in my ear, one that

matches my own heartbeat. "Yes, I want to come. For you, Kingston, for you …"

"Rub your clit, love. Faster. Think of me touching you, pulling your body to the brink of release." I'm caught in it now, the tingle of my impending climax hurdling down my spine and into my balls.

"Yes, yes … oh my …" Poppy lets out a harsh cry, and I know she's coming.

The last image I see in my brain before it goes hazy with pleasure is one of her arched back on the bed, her lips forming an O as the orgasm wracks her body.

Every muscle in my body tenses as cum shoots from my tip, coating my hand and boxers. The sheer force of pleasure makes me grind my teeth together, a hoarse, almost silent groan leaving my lips.

It takes a few seconds for my vision to come back into focus, for the warm lull of pleasure to lift from my body.

"Wow," Poppy says, and I realize her voice is so far away because I dropped the phone into the sofa cushions.

Picking it up, a cheeky grin spreads across my face. "Well, now, wasn't that better than unclogging the sink?"

A giggle in my ear. "Normally, I would make some remark about how you're an arrogant scoundrel. But, I'm too content and knackered to be that quick-witted, so I'll just agree. Yes, that was *loads* better than unclogging the sink."

27

POPPY

As if Kingston worked some kind of magic, the intimacy we shared over the phone has unlocked something inside of me.

Not only did I give my trust over to a man, allowing him to affect my body and its reactions, but he held that responsibility so sacredly that I feel a shift. My heart is lighter. For five years, I've felt a kind of pressure bearing down on the organ. But the way Kingston has delicately helped me through my fears and has a desire to see me comfortable in this relationship ...

It makes me want to afford him the same trust.

I wasn't planning on telling him the story of what happened to me when I was fifteen, but then I saw him get out of the elevator mere minutes ago, and I just knew. I took one look at him, this incredible man with a heart of gold that he hid under pranks and sarcasm, and I knew that I was about to confess everything.

The trip back to London is supposed to be a happy one. We're celebrating the victory of Nartanica making it into the fourth tier championship, all thanks to Kingston. If they win the match, it could mean very good things for the future of his football career. According to him, the manager at RFC has been keeping tabs on his progress and is cautiously impressed with the hard work he's putting in.

But as we enter my flat and Kingston shrugs his duffle bag off to head straight for me, I hold a hand up.

"I need to ... I want to tell you." It's so sudden that my voice feels foreign to my own ears.

At first, he doesn't understand. "Tell me what, babe?"

"I want to tell you. I couldn't before, but ... I trust you, Kingston." I raise my eyebrows, trying to subtly suggest that this is a big moment between us.

His features mold into shock, but he schools them, trying for attentive and compassionate. "If you are ready, then I am here to listen."

I appreciate that he doesn't ask me if I'm sure. Kingston just allows me to make the decision, and doesn't persuade me one way or the other.

"Let's sit." My hands fidget, and immediately I begin to regret the idea.

What if I misspoke, or acted too soon? He will look at me differently after this. What if he doubts it happened, or if he questions why I never told the authorities?

But now he's looking at me, eyes trained on mine and one hand holding onto my fingers for moral support.

So I jump, falling into the story the only way I know how and steeling myself for the emotional torment I know will come.

"When I was fifteen, I was asked to shoot a campaign for a very high-profile brand. It was the first time I really thought I was making it in this business, especially because they'd signed a world-renowned photographer. Nicolai DeCallen."

I have to stop because just saying his name makes me want to hyperventilate.

"When I arrived, everyone was so welcoming. Especially

him, praising my work and telling me how wonderful it was to work with me. We got right to business; hair, makeup, clothes, the works. And then the shoot got underway, and it was incredible. So innovative, and the shots were just beautiful. Nicolai called a midday break, and most of the staff went out to get lunch, but he said he wanted to talk through the shoot more with me, so I joined him in the makeshift office he had in the studio. He gave me a glass of wine, told me it would help me relax ... move the process along. I was fifteen and still very new in the industry, that Feraldo campaign was the biggest thing to ever happen to me in my life. I'd done small shoots, group magazine stuff, and some editorial work. But this? It was a major fashion house asking me to be their feature model. Of course, I wanted to act like I was an experienced professional, and like I drank wine all the time. In reality, that was the first glass of red I'd ever sipped."

I shudder just thinking about it, and how I've never been able to stomach a cabernet or merlot since.

My eyes are averted, looking at a spot on the floor, because I know if I look at Kingston, I'll break down. I have to get through this, recite it in machine-like fashion, or I'll never be able to tell the entire story.

"After a few sips, I began to feel strange. My limbs felt fuzzy, sluggish. My speech began slurring, and after a few more seconds, I started to panic. I clawed at his arm, trying to tell him that I thought I was dying or having a heart attack, or something. I was fully conscious when he slipped his hand beneath my shirt, when he touched my nipples and invaded my personal space. The drugs only rendered my limbs unusable, but my brain was fully aware when he—"

Breaking off in a sob that breaks the lump of emotion in my throat, I will myself to go on. I've never told anyone about this, never uttered the words. As long as I could keep moving, lock it away in an airtight box in the back of my brain, I would be okay. Or so I thought.

"He put his fingers inside me. It hurt so much I tried to cry out for help, but my vocal cords were paralyzed from both the drugs and the fear. I'm not sure what he was trying to do, and I could barely move my neck, but I know he was touching himself. It felt like years that he assaulted me, that he stole my innocence and ruined any normal relationship I'd have with my body, with sex, with men. Do you know what I thought after he was finished? At least he didn't rape me. Fuck, how foolish I'd been. Of course, he raped me. Maybe not in the literal sense, but he's stolen everything from me. And the worst part of it all? I went back out there and finished the shoot. Dragged myself from the room he'd left me in, blood tinging my underwear, and stood in front of the camera while he emotionally assaulted me from behind it."

I can't say anymore, my vocal cords so strung out and fried from the unshed tears. It takes a minute or two until he finally speaks.

"I'll kill him." Kingston's voice is so deadly quiet, I'm afraid he's going to hurl one of my couches out of the penthouse-story window.

"Kingston, no." I'm desperate as I clutch his arm. "No one can ever know about this. I've never told another soul ... I can't bring myself to. It would only result in my name being spread everywhere, associated with this evil thing. My tragedy would be used as magazine fodder, and who knows if they'd even take action against him? He's far more powerful than either of us know, of that I'm sure. I'd be labeled a victim, the public would pity me. I've never wanted that. And what happens if they don't? What happens if they label me a fame whore or a phony? Women everywhere allow men to do things they're not comfortable with because it's easier than putting up a fight. It's simpler than being labeled or ridiculed. And I was one of them. I let a grown man sexually assault me at the age of fifteen, and because he was behind the photo shoot that launched my career, I'd kept my mouth shut. I told no one that an adult put his hands on me, that he took something I'd never get back, just so I could make money and be catapulted into fame."

In an instant, Kingston has my face in his hands, his eyes boring holes into mine. "I don't ever want to hear those words come out of your mouth again. You didn't *let* anyone do anything to you. A grown man drugged and assaulted you, took away your consent. Don't even let me hear you imply that you were complicit in it. Secondly, nothing that happened before or after was your fault in any way. You were *fifteen*, Poppy! You had no one guiding you, no one you trusted enough to confide in. You were a scared, shocked girl, no one can judge or ridicule the way you acted after. I ... fuck, I'm so angry I want to hit something."

My eyes widen because he has my jaw in his palms. He must sense my fear, because he softens his features, his thumbs stroking my cheeks.

"Poppy, no. Never. I will only ever protect you. I'm not angry with you, I'm angry at the universe that let this happen to a fifteen-year-old girl. I'm furious at the man who took advantage of you, who abused his power. There is nothing more I want than to give what he took back to you, but I know I can't."

My heart soars, even though I just admitted the ugliest part of me. I shared my truth, all the prickly, horrible parts of it, and Kingston only wants to console me. He wants to erase my pain, and ...

There is nothing more I want than for him to take away those memories and replace them with ones of him.

"You can, Kingston. Touch me."

28

POPPY

The uncertainty in his clover-green eyes makes me even more certain that we were always meant to find each other.

"Love, this was a lot for you to process. I don't want to cloud this moment with something physical, that you might not want—"

I cut him off, feeling more empowered than I have in five years. I don't ask him if he wants me, if his rebuff has to do with him not wanting to be with me. Because I know it's not. Instead, I pick my strength up by its bootstraps and take what I want. The confidence that fled when I was fifteen is back in full force, seeming to have returned when I let my secret out of the terrifying box I'd been keeping it in.

"Kingston, I know how monumental this is. And I know that I shared a very dark part of myself. But make no mistake, I know exactly what I want. I want you to fill me up with light, to show me how things are supposed to feel in a sexy, steamy, intimate relationship. I want you to be a man, and me to be a woman, and for us to do the things our bodies naturally want to do to each other. I'm not scared anymore, I'm not cowering or unsure. This is what I want."

He takes only a moment, to inhale and exhale, before taking me by both of my hands and walking to my bedroom. It's early, the daylight coming in through the open window, and part of me wants to cower with how exposed I will be. But this is how it should be. I want Kingston to see all of me, and I want to see all of him.

Without talking, there has been too much of that today, Kingston begins to undress me. Slowly, with care, he pulls the simple sundress over my head, revealing the unlined bra and matching panties beneath. My skin pebbles with goose bumps, and his tongue darts out to make a sexy swipe of his lip. I arch my back when he runs a hand down my bare arm, my body pressing into his. The moment the skin of my torso touches his T-shirt, I want it off.

So, I pull it over his head. This man has shown me nothing but kindness, an open dialogue, and caution. There is something heady about that combination that's making me brazen. Kingston's naked abdomen, something I've only seen in glimpses before now, is something out of a woman's wildest fantasy. He has muscles on his muscles, each groove carved into his stomach begs to be traced and licked. The V of the corded muscles that dip beneath his boxers sends a tingle down my spine.

My bedroom is silent, and there is something unspoken between us. We're going to revel in the quiet and find each other between the brushes of skin and sighs.

I run my fingers along the ridges of his muscles, over his abs and up to his collarbone, where I fan out and scrape my nails down his biceps. Kingston lets out a ragged groan, and his hands gently grip my wrists, moving them away from his body and walking me backward until my knees buckle. I fall onto the bed, and the man gives me a look as if to say, "Oh, you foolish woman."

There is no way he's letting me have full control. And I'm shocked to find, I don't want it. I don't need it. Actually, I'm buzzing with anticipation as he maneuvers me.

Kingston uses what looks like an ounce of his strength to move me up the bed, my head connecting with the pillows. He follows me, moving with the grace of a jungle cat, and his hands find the soft cotton of my bra. Pulling the cups down until I spring free, he doesn't give me a moment to doubt. A wet mouth comes down on one nipple, and my hips shoot up, the electricity flowing from the sensitive bud Kingston is sucking at straight down to the live wire between my thighs.

Moving to the other, he uses his teeth and lips, teasing me until I'm panting and writhing. Who knew a man could bring you so much pleasure simply from touching your breasts?

I'm so close to that ever-elusive peak, the one I have only managed to reach a couple of times alone. But Kingston hadn't even touched me when I'd come from our phone sex session, so it was no wonder he could get me dangerously close to climax in no time at all.

Reaching for him, he bats my hand away and shakes his head. I knew he was going to focus on me but all the attention feels undeserved. I'm not used to a man being so respectful of me or my body.

Without letting up, Kingston kisses down my torso, licking at my navel and then going lower. When he gets to the band of my underwear, he uses his teeth to pull at the elastic, moving them down my hips. Dear God, this man is a sex master.

I can't catch my breath as I watch him undress me, the hot and cold flushes through my system throwing me completely off balance.

My legs are shaking by the time Kingston positions his face

between them and bites his bottom lip. His eyes are molten as he flicks them up to mine, and with his gaze on mine, he lowers his mouth and plunges his tongue into my center.

Everything in me explodes like one giant firework. White dots cloud my vision as Kingston uses his tongue to penetrate me. It feels so exquisite, I'm not even sure I'm fully in control of my own muscles.

It's when his teeth clamp down on my sensitive nub that I go off like a rocket.

My mouth forms an O, but no sound comes out as I give into the orgasm ... the most powerful one I've ever had.

Only one thought prevails as my entire system ripples with the effects of my climax:

Kingston Phillips is not who I thought he was, and I'm falling head over heels for the man I've found him to be.

29

KINGSTON

"Blimey, it's hot."

I check the weather app on my mobile and see that it's going to still be eighty degrees at almost ten o'clock.

Poppy doesn't stir from where she lies on my chest, the sounds of the telly in the background. She's been watching some chick flick with Matthew McConaughey for about an hour while I scroll through Twitter, checking up on my favorite football analysts and trying to gauge how this weekend's Nartanica championship is being weighted.

To say I'm nervous about the match would be an understatement. That's probably a good sign since I've never cared much about a regular match or one that could bring trophies. I never cared much about anything, until I thought I lost it all. The fact that I'm anxious about playing well, about bringing glory to the squad that accepted me at my lowest ... I just want to do right by them.

This weekend has been everything it was supposed to be and more. I'd decided to come to London for a few days to get things off my mind. Funny, I used to think of this city as the playground for my playboy antics, but now, it holds the one person who is an escape for me. Being with Poppy, having a person who understands you at a molecular level, that's what all the fuss about relationships is about. I never realized it until I found her.

"Oh, yeah?" she says distractedly, popping a cherry tomato in her mouth.

"Jesus, how do you eat those things?" I pretend to cringe.

They're her favorite snack, which I don't understand. My favorite snack is chips or popcorn or a big ice cream sundae. Cherry tomatoes, I'll never understand it.

"I love them, so live with it, mate."

"I'm not your mate. Do you let your mates stick their tongue between your thighs?" My large hand squeezes one of her curvy hips.

She giggles and squirms away. "Definitely not."

"Righto. Now, I have an idea on how to combat this heat wave."

Her sapphire eyes meet mine. "And what's that?"

"Have you ever checked out the rooftop pool?" My grin is cheeky and suspicious.

It seemed daft to me, when I first bought my flat at Charlton House, that a London residence would have an outdoor pool. We don't have that many warm days, and it seemed very Los Angeles or Santorini to me. But then I'd gone up for winter swims, realizing it was heated, and the novelty of it was not lost on me. It was quite beautiful up there with the freezing temperatures surrounding the heated pool.

"Once or twice. Why?" Poppy is focusing on her movie again.

I shift, managing to slide out from under her cuddle and stand. She shifts, landing in an awkward position on the couch.

"Hey! I was very comfortable." She pouts.

"And you're about to be way more comfortable. With me. Upstairs." I make a move to grab her keys and slide on my shoes.

"Kingston, it's late. I'm tired. Why do we have to go upstairs?" she whines.

"Just trust me. You'll really enjoy this." I hold my hand out to help her off the sofa, and after a brief pause, she laces her fingers in mine and allows me to lead her.

We enter the elevator and I push the button for the roof, turning to her and winking. "What we're about to do is really going to fluff Mrs. Clemens feathers."

And then I proceed to pull the shirt I'm wearing up and over my head.

"Kingston! What are you—"

Poppy can't finish her sentence, because I push my gym shorts past my hips, letting them fall to the floor of the lift.

"*Oh, no* ... absolutely not ..." She holds her hands up as I back her into the corner.

"Come on, love. Come skinny dipping with me." My voice is pure devilish amusement.

She shakes that gorgeous head of hers furiously. "No! What if someone comes up to the roof? Or sees us from one of the other buildings. Imagine the papers getting a hold of that!"

I run my hands up and down her arm. "Only the top two floors have access, and no one is coming up here this late. Charlton House is the highest building in Belgravia, so that point is moot. Any other concerns? Live a little, Miss Raymond."

Poppy does not stop trying to push me away and shaking her head. "You're mental. Put your clothes on!"

The lift doors ding, letting us know we've arrived on the roof, and I wink. "Too late!"

And with that, I sprint from the lift, stumbling to shuck my boxers off before running to the pool and jumping in.

"Kingston!" I hear Poppy screech and then giggle right before I hit the water.

The contrast of the humid night and the cool, refreshing

water slicking over my skin makes me feel alive. I let myself sink all the way to the bottom of the pool and then kick up when my toes hit the cement.

I'm treading water, shaking the drops out of my hair, when Poppy reaches the side and crosses her arms, looking down at me.

"Come on in, the water feels fine." I grin up at her.

"You're *mad*." She laughs.

"And you love it. Now get your beautiful arse in this pool." I splash her, dotting her shirt with water.

"Hey! Not fair. And what if someone comes up?"

I shrug, still treading. "Then they get to see two of the most gorgeous humans on earth swimming in the nude."

Something flashes in her eyes, I think it's recklessness, and before I can ask her again, Poppy is stepping out of her lounge clothes.

It's quite the show, all of those long limbs and perfectly sculpted curves. I have to swim into the shallow end just to stay afloat with the way her undressing is affecting me.

With a brazen smile, Poppy marches to the diving board, walks down it, quickly pulls off her bra and underwear, and then dives flawlessly into the water. Her entrance barely makes a splash, and I watch as she swims all the way under the water until she reaches me.

When she comes up, the wetness sluices down her body and face, creating some kind of epic fantasy that every man should bear witness to. Except that this is mine, and I'm not sharing.

I grab her by the waist, floating us until my back is pressed against the cement wall and every part of her is nestled against every part of me.

"See? Didn't I tell you this was a great idea?" I bite playfully at the tip of her nose.

Poppy reaches down and wraps her hand around my cock,

which has been hard since she dove in. "Yes, this was a really good idea."

I'm so shocked, and turned on, that I have to keep my head straight to be a gentleman. "Poppy, you don't have to ..."

She tugs at my shaft, testing out a few strokes. I have to grip the edge of the pool to keep myself from bloody drowning.

"I never returned the favor yesterday. And I have a lot of things I want to try when it comes to this part of you."

The way Poppy says it, so naively yet so confidently at the same time, nearly gives me a heart attack.

And then she reaches down to put her other hand on my balls, and I can't think anymore.

30

KINGSTON

We won. We bloody won.

Donnie raises the trophy over his head, the one that marks Nartanica as fourth-tier champions of the year.

And to my shock, I'm more proud of this accomplishment than I've ever been of anything. When I was first demoted and sent here, I thought it was a death sentence. This was the place where my career came to die, of that I was sure. I'd mourned what could have been until the guys who have become my good mates in the short months I've been playing here put me in my place.

I'm not sure I would have come as far if Donnie, Finnegan, and the blokes hadn't treated me just like any other player. Their lack of enthusiasm about my arrival helped me to realize just how much I love this game. Being forced to struggle through the work, to re-dedicate myself, to fight for my position on the pitch, it opened my eyes to just how much I did want this to be my life, and my legacy.

Today, when I stepped out onto the grass, smelling the

same scent I've relished since the day I started walking, it all clicked into place. I am ready to accept my role in this game, in its history, in the victory of the squad I played for.

"Not bad, Phillips. Not bad!" Donnie envelops me in a bear hug.

"Wahoo!" Finnegan whoops as he hits us full force, his body joining in on the celebratory gesture. He ruffles my hair. "You're going straight to the top after this. Good job, boyo."

My heart thuds against my rib cage, and the hope I've been trying to tamp down springs eternal.

After the victory celebration, in which we race around the Narta stadium doing laps with the trophy over our heads, we head to the locker room and pop open a few bottles of champagne. My teammates spray it in showers, cheering and talking about the future and how they were going to fly to Paris to celebrate. I enjoy the festivities with them, taking the time to slow down and bask in the jubilation.

Then I shower, don a comfortable outfit of jeans and a T-shirt, and shoulder my backpack.

Pulling out my mobile, there are four missed texts from Poppy.

Poppy: *Oh my God! You won!*

Poppy: *I am so proud of you, babe.*

Poppy: *We are for sure celebrating when I get home from Los Angeles.*

Poppy: *This was always your destiny, Kingston. I hope you know that. I'm so happy for you.*

She's in LA for a meeting with a brand, something about an exclusive product they want her to market, and wasn't able to come to the game. But, my girlfriend is a boss and I didn't mind. Celebrating the victory afterward with her, preferably on one of our beds, would more than make up for it.

Kingston: *Thanks, love. I can't wait to see you. I miss you. Probably be falling asleep soon here, hope your meeting is going well.*

Waiting a few minutes, I don't see any indication that she read the message or is typing, so I push the phone into my pocket and head out. A bunch of the guys are still partying in the locker room, but I'm knackered.

When I walk out, into the halls of the Narta building, I'm truly stunned at who is standing in the hallway before me.

"Brilliant match, Kingston." Niles Harrington is leaning against the wall and pushes off when he sees me nearing.

"Niles, I didn't know you'd be here." I'm a little out of my element here, completely thrown off guard by him showing up.

"That was a bit of the point. I wanted to see what you'd do if there wasn't anything riding on this match." His usual chilly demeanor is in place.

The bloke has always kind of spooked me, and not only because he held my career in his hands. Niles Harrington always seems two or three steps ahead of anyone else, and I've always secretly thought he could read minds. Every time I speak, it's like he sees right through whatever it is I'm trying to feed him.

"And what did you think, sir?" Did I just drop a sir? Who was I?

"My frustration with you was never over your match play. You're extremely gifted, Kingston. My problem was your attitude. You have all of this talent that you were wasting, and as not only a coach but a person ... it's bloody hard to watch. You made it acceptable to the other players on my squad to slack off; I had to put my fist down. And for your benefit too, I could see you struggling with your place in this world. Do you want it bad enough? Are you willing to put in one hundred and twenty percent of the effort being at this level takes?"

His words sink in, and I nod slowly. "When you loaned me

out, I hated you. I was surly and arrogant, and you're right, I had no idea if I really wanted to play football. But being here taught me that I love this game regardless of what it means to be a Phillips."

Niles nods, his eyes cutting sharply to mine. A beat passes, my future hanging in the air between us.

"Come back to Rogue. You passed the test, you proved yourself. There will be a car waiting outside of your hotel, we'll need you back for practice tomorrow so get packed and head to London. Oh, and Kingston, no more need to measure up to who your father wants you to be. He might be considered one of the best to ever play, but I always thought he had rather dodgy footwork."

He doesn't want an answer, because there is only one I could honestly give. I'd never turn his offer down, he knows that. It's why Niles walks off silently into the dark corridor, not waiting to hear what I have to say.

And that line he slipped in about my father? Blimey, it seems I've underestimated my manager.

I barely have time to process the last five minutes, save the last few hours. In a heartbeat, I'm moving toward the car, being driven to my hotel, packing up, and heading to London. I text Donnie and Finnegan, telling them the news, and that I'll try to get back for one of their games soon. It's a whirlwind, and there are about a hundred things to think about, but I'll never forget what those blokes have done for me.

The drive back to London sees me trying to ring Poppy about seven times, to no success. Where she is, I have no idea, and I feel like I might burst with the news if I don't tell someone soon. I text Jude, though he's probably sleeping since it is the middle of the night. Although, I don't tell him I'm coming back to Rogue. It will be hilarious to see the look on his face when I show up to practice tomorrow.

Finally, the car stops in front of Charlton House, the streets of Belgravia quiet. I wave to the night receptionist and make my way to the lifts, toting my two bags with me. It will be bloody heaven sleeping on my expensive mattress fitted with expensive sheets. That's one thing I've missed about London, maybe even more than the twenty four hour service industry waiting to give you whatever you desire. Do you want pad thai at three a.m.? They've got you covered.

As if this night couldn't get any stranger, there is another person standing in a hallway waiting for me.

"What are you doing here?" It's well past a decent time of night, and there should be no reason he'd want to talk to me anyway.

"I wanted to make sure you got home." He pushes off the wall, the bulk of him settling onto the floor with a grunt.

"Dear old Dad, finally caring about me. Never thought I'd see the day." Sarcasm drips from my tone as I turn to face my father.

"I wanted to make sure you were home so that you got a good night of rest and didn't embarrass the Phillips name tomorrow. You've mucked up enough for your mother and I and you've gotten a second chance. Don't squander it."

Ah, there he is, the mean old bastard I know and didn't even remotely like. "Thanks for the brilliant pep talk. Now get out of my building."

How had he even gotten up here in the first place?

"Don't disrespect me. I'm your father, I've given you everything you have in this life. This flat? Bought with money I helped supply you with, in one way or another. My blood runs in your veins, that talent you have is a gift from me!"

My father is so irate, there is spit gathering at the corners of his mouth, as if he's a rabid animal. I think he can tell I've finally reached the point where I'm free from his ridicule. Something happened to me in Nartanica, and perhaps that was the realization that I can walk out from under his boot whenever I bloody please.

"Whatever the genetics of yours running in my veins, those are the ones that have poisoned me for twenty-one years. The ones that made me believe I'd never measure up. The voice of doubt in my head causing me to waste so much time wondering if I could be a bloody Phillips. And now I know ... I don't have to be any part of you. I am *me*. Kingston. It doesn't matter what surname is on the back of my kit, it's the man wearing it and how he conducts himself that matters. And I conduct myself loads better than you ever have."

"You foul little git." My father advances on me, pinning me to the wall opposite my front door and leaning in hard with his elbow on my neck.

It doesn't escape me that with one swift blow to the temple, I could overpower him.

"What are you going to do? Choke me? Hit me? Go ahead, your words, along with your actions, mean nothing anymore," I taunt him, cursing him as he holds my throat in his clutches.

Because it's true, he can't touch me anymore. Not on an emotional level, that is. I know who I am, and he can no longer affect me.

By some grace of God, the lift doors open, and out walks the woman who has managed to change me in every way possible.

"What are you ... how?" Momentarily, I forget my father is there, because I'm so shocked to see her.

Her aqua irises flick to my father pinning my against the wall. Her eyes go ice cold, but she answers my question anyway. "I decided to leave early. I was going to try to surprise you in Nartanica tomorrow. But I'm glad I caught you here."

My father takes his hands off me, jumping back as if all of

Scotland Yard's forces just came up to the penthouse floor. He never could stand to have his image tainted, even if he was a monster inside his own home. Smile for the cameras and remain upstanding citizens to the public, that was his number one priority.

Smoothing my shirt where he rumpled it, I pick up my bags, walking to my door. Poppy meets me there, wrapping her arms around my waist and pressing her body to mine. Just having her here, feeling the warmth bleeding through our respective clothing ... it comforts me in a way I never realized I needed before.

"Get out of here. And don't come back. I don't want to see you at my matches. If you show up, I'll have stadium security ban you. Don't make me do that, I know how you love keeping your image tidy."

"You daft twi—"

Poppy cuts him off, her voice stony. "He told you to leave."

While my father has strength on his side, Poppy has about a foot on him, his Italian stature more short and stocky than long and lean. I get my build from my mother. It's comical to see my girlfriend tower over my father, a glare on her face as she peers down her nose at him.

"What is this? Your pussy protection squad?" My father practically spits.

"Yes. And her bite is meaner than her bark. Leave." I stare him down.

After a second or two, he huffs off, jabbing the button for the lift. When it arrives, he marches in, sending one last glare over his shoulder as the doors close.

I let out the breath I've been holding and drop my bags, pulling Poppy in tighter and burying my nose in her hair.

"Blimey, am I glad to see you." I hold her close.

"I'm so proud of you," she whispers.

And I know she's not just talking about being asked to return to RFC. No, she means that I finally stood up for myself and the fact that Poppy knows how monumental that is speaks volumes about how deep the relationship between us really is.

31

POPPY

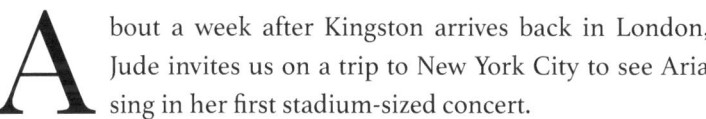

About a week after Kingston arrives back in London, Jude invites us on a trip to New York City to see Aria sing in her first stadium-sized concert.

And to celebrate the end of football season. Not that football is ever over, the blokes have an international friendly in three short weeks, but the break is sport wide and allows the players to get some rest and relaxation.

I have to fly in separately from Milan, where I am walking in a runway show for an Italian brand, but I'm happy to do it. I haven't gotten much face time with Kingston's friends, and this might be the trip where we all bond and become mates. While I love spending alone time with Kingston, I've never had a *group*. I've never had friends who included me in their plans, or a boyfriend to go on double dates with our couple friends. It seems so normal, almost like we're living the real lives of twentysomethings, rather than the ridiculous ones we actually do. I'll take all the normal I can get.

As for seeing Aria in concert, I'm excited. The first album she released last year has become one of my go-to listens when I travel or drive, and her voice is spellbinding. She was asked to open up for a high-profile pop singer, and while I know she's nervous, she's also going to be smashing.

The four of us are in the back of a limo, driving through the crowded, bustling streets of arguably the most notorious city on earth, and so far, the trip has been amazing. We've only been here a day, but we spent it lounging on a blanket in Central Park for lunch, and then Aria and I did some damage to our credit cards on the streets of New York, while the men went to tour Yankee Stadium. I convinced her to buy a slinky silver dress at Saks, while I picked up a sheer white coat at Bergdorf Goodman I've been eyeing for months.

It's eight p.m., but by the way this city shines, you'd never know it. Times Square is lit up like a disco ball, and everywhere you look there are sounds and smells. I live in one of the biggest cities in the world, but nothing compares to the Big Apple. This place, every crevice and corner of it, is simply ... *alive*.

"I can't wait to eat, I'm starving!" Kingston whines and rubs his stomach which I know for a fact is something carved of stone.

"You're always starving." Aria rolls her eyes at him. "One time, I had these blokes over to my row home in Clavering ... Kingston ate almost an entire roast chicken, and then asked for a third helping of pudding at dessert!"

"Doesn't surprise." I chuckle. "He lives right next door and inevitably comes over to raid my entire pantry."

"I raid more than that." He nuzzles into my neck, tickling me and I squirm while a blush ravages my cheeks.

"Leave Poppy alone, she's far too classy for your innuendos. There is a chef's kitchen at Madison Square Garden, apparently, they'll even hand roll sushi for you." Jude rubs his hands together.

"I don't think I'll be able to eat a morsel, I'm so nervous ...

what if I'm booed off stage?" Aria looks a little green, and her boyfriend reaches over to clasp her hand in his.

But I'm the one who interjects. "Are you joking? You're going to smash it! It's okay to be nervous, I was before every single one of my early runway shows. But don't be nervous about your own talent. I swear, Aria, you're my favorite artist right now. I wouldn't just say that to blow smoke, you know that. I'm honest—"

"And harsh, so you know you can trust her opinion when she compliments you." Kingston nods emphatically.

"He's right. I've been known to be a bitch. But about your performance, I'm not bluffing."

She tips her head, smiling at me in thanks, but I can tell she's still uneasy. "How are you all so calm when you have to go out there in front of people? I swear, I'll never get used to it."

Kingston shrugs. "Eh, just picture everyone naked, love."

"Is that what you do? Picture the sniveling, enormous, ruddy blokes nude in the stands during matches?" Jude cackles.

"Prick." Kingston smacks the back of Jude's head.

I reach across the limo to squeeze Aria's hand.

We arrive at Madison Square Garden, the humongous circular structure built into the side of New York's Penn Station teaming with lights and fans and vendors hocking street food. It's glorious, and the four of us are shown to a private entrance where we're then led to a hallway of dressing rooms.

"Oh my God, my name is on the door," Aria squeals, and I'm excited for her.

I've been doing things like this my whole young adult life, but I remember when the newness hadn't yet worn off. When every moment seemed extraordinary and it was as if everything you dreamed of was coming true. It was a beautiful thing to view it through another's eyes.

A hair and makeup team come in and start working on Aria,

and the boys go off to find food. I stay in the background as Aria's manager gives her pointers, and only speak up when there is a lull and I have a small piece of encouragement to give.

An hour and a half later, it's time for her to go on. She's wearing these fabulous knee-high crushed velvet boots paired with a romper that is both sophisticated and fun. It's exactly the type of outfit I would have picked for her first show.

The microphone in her hand is shaking with nerves as she peeks through the curtains hiding us from the view of thousands.

"Blimey, that's a lot of people."

I correct her. "A lot of *fans*. These people came here to see you. Just be yourself, sing the words you put to paper."

"Or don't, and they'll throw tomatoes at you," Kingston quips, and I give him a murderous glare.

But Aria just laughs. "No, actually, that might be better. Heckle me before I get on stage, it'll take the edge off."

I grin. "In that case, you have a terrible voice and are a mean girl."

"Hey, don't spread that codswallop about my daughter."

Aria whips around, the biggest smile stretching across her face.

"Dad? DAD! What are you doing here? Oh my God!" Aria runs to him, flinging herself into her father's arms and then turning to look at Jude. "Did you know about this?"

"Who do you think convinced him to get on a plane?" Jude laughs, walking over to shake Aria's father's hand.

My smile is a mix of jubilation for Aria—I know how close she and her father are and it's nice that he traveled all this way for her first American show—but it's tinged with bitterness, for a relationship I'll never know with my parents.

When I turn to lean into Kingston because I could use an extra hug right now, he's no longer standing next to me.

I whip around, watching as the door to the stage slams closed. My heart sinks, because I have a feeling why Kingston just bolted.

It takes me a few minutes, and I'm a hundred percent sure I'm lost in the maze of this arena, but I eventually find my boyfriend sitting against a wall near a bank of golf carts used to quickly zip around the place.

Gingerly, I join him, making sure to sit so that our knees brush, but not moving to touch him with my hands.

"I should have told you something when you confessed to me about your assault." Kingston ducks his head, and I see him chewing on the inside of his cheek.

My mind flashes back to that day in the cafe with Aria and what she told me. As if I have a sixth sense, I already know what Kingston is about to divulge. I am not going to tell him I already knew ... no, that would serve no purpose. Plus, I only know the information from Aria's account of it. He deserves to have me sit next to him, holding his hand, while he recounts it to me.

"Last night, in the hallway ... that wasn't the first time my father put his hands on me. It's not been an often occurrence, but it's not rare either. Before I was recruited for the Rogue Academy, so before my seventh birthday, it was just verbal abuse. I don't mean to say just, God knows that stuck in my mind far more than his punches, slaps, or yanks ever did. All of it ... it leaves behind marks, but it also leaves behind this emotional trauma you can never wipe clean. As hard as I try, I can never rub the stain of it off my soul. Why can't my parents be normal? Why can't they love me, like that? Fly halfway across the world just because they're proud of what I've accomplished. Bloody hell, I don't mean to be a whiny twit, but I have *never* gotten one ounce of the love Aria gets from her dad, from my father. And because of it, I'm all fucked up. It's taken years to be able to express my emotions properly, but before that, I was riding around on top of limousines just to get attention. I almost threw my career away. I shut myself off so brutally that I almost lost out on the chance to be with you."

Not able to contain my restless hands anymore, I wrap my arms around his shoulders and cradle him into me, kissing his hair as I speak into it.

"You are a lion, Kingston, as regal as the animals gracing the crest of the league you love so dearly. You are loyal and fiercely passionate about what you want to protect. But you also have a temper that gets you in trouble, and you don't walk on anyone's leash. You're the ruler of your kingdom, and you're unforgiving when someone wrongs you. These are the qualities I admire most in you. There is nothing wrong with guarding your heart with brute force."

He stays tucked into me.

"I don't want to guard my heart, at least not from you. What I've realized over the past few months is that you and me? We're the same. Both victims of what this privileged, horrible, tragic world has done to us. But we rise above it. Watching you get up every day and go to work, despite what happened to you ... it's inspiring. I want to be better. You make me want to be better."

"Together. You and I are better *together*."

32

KINGSTON

Clavering hasn't changed a bit.

As Jude winds his Maserati through the streets of the small town we attended football academy in, a sense of longing burns in my chest. While I loathed school, every part of it besides the football, this was my home for many, many years of my life.

It's the place where I first walked onto the Rogue Academy campus, where I envisioned myself training to become one of the best football players in history. The Rogue Academy is where I met Jude and Vance for the first time, where we became brothers and had each other's backs through it all.

Out of the passenger-side window, the spires of the academy come into view, and suddenly we're upon it, winding through the old church-like buildings and straight up to our old dorm. Ah, how many girls did we sneak in here? How many pranks did we pull? Yes, I'd missed this place, and it is good to be back.

When Jude suggested we take a drive to the academy after coming back from New York, I didn't hesitate. Vance hadn't been able to come on the trip, and I felt bloody awful about that.

"Vance, brother!" I bound out of the car, scooping my most

solemn friend up into a massive hug.

"Blimey, watch my back, King. I've been working dive saves all day and I feel like a bunch of broken glass," Vance complains.

"How'd they go?" Jude asks, shaking his hand and clapping him on the shoulder.

"Smashing. Not that it matters. I'll be stuck here until the end of time." He says this as if it's a fact.

I feel bloody awful for my friend. He is a brilliant keeper, but his position at RFC is a catch twenty-two. They won't promote him to the first squad because Remus is incredible, just a hair better than Vance. But, the higher-ups won't sell him because one, he'd be an amazing backup if Remus got injured. And two, when Remus does eventually retire, they'll bring Vance up. It's not fair to waste so many years of his talent, but this is the business of football.

"Mate, you won't. You're going to get your shot. Or you'll end up in Narta, like Kingston." Jude slaps him on the back, trying to make light of the situation.

Vance doesn't smile, and I scowl. "Hey, I busted my arse to prove myself again."

Jude makes a *pshh* sound as if what I'm saying is just codswallop.

"All right, so what are we pulling tonight?" I ask, rubbing my palms together.

We got into a lot of shenanigans when we all went to academy here, and now that we were back, I was feeling the urge to commit mischief.

"King, I still live here. Don't shite where I sleep." Vance rolls his eyes at me.

"We're here to hang out. No mucking anything up." Jude points his finger at me.

"I am still London's greatest prankster. I wouldn't be Kingston Phillips if we didn't pull one over on someone. I might be new and improved, but come on, I still need my jokes from time to time." I lay the charm on thick, trying to get Jude to budge.

His eyes are shifty and nervous, but I can see the moment he finally relents. "Okay, fine. But nothing dangerous, and only slightly illegal. I'm not jumping off the roof again or setting off fireworks in the parking lot!"

"Got it. I know just the thing."

Headmaster Darnot is the reigning ruler of Rogue Football Academy, the place where we all grew up together. And he's a daft wanker if I've ever seen one. Responsible for almost all the rubbish I'd been given by my parents as a boy, he had no sense of humor and even less of a tolerance for me than Poppy did in the beginning. Every prank I pulled, each stunt on the pitch or in the classroom, Darnot handed me my arse.

Well, I am all grown up now, and it's time to get one last sweet piece of revenge.

"Where the hell did you get this idea? And how did you know how to rig it so quickly? Why do I feel like you've been planning this for a long time?" Vance asks, a confused look on his face.

We're in Darnot's office, where I'm stringing up the last of the prank and Jude and Vance survey my handiwork. My plan has come along quite nicely, and even I'm shocked that it's worked as well as I thought it would.

"Have neither of you seen *The Parent Trap*? The one with Lindsay Lohan where one of her has a British accent? She's quite good, almost sounds like a natural Londoner—"

"Kingston, focus. I don't need to know about Disney movies for preteen girls."

"Right, anyway, she pranks the rival cabin at her sleep away camp, and this is how she does it. Bloody brilliant, right? Of course, Vance, you're going to have to get pictures for us somehow. This will only be a smash if I can have physical proof of Darnot with feathers and chocolate sauce all over his face."

"And how am I supposed to do that?" Vance scowls, the big guy growing more annoyed by the second.

"Figure it out! I'm going to be like a schoolgirl, almost wetting her knickers until you text me a photo." I point a finger at him.

"I kind of have a little more than taking prank pictures on my plate. But thanks for asking." He glares at me and then walks off down the hall, his footsteps echoing in the dark, empty corridor.

Jude and I exchange a look like we knew he was bound to blow up at any second. On the same breath, we both hightail it out of the office, being careful to shut and lock the door and then chase after our friend.

When we reach him, Vance is sitting on the floor with his back against a glass case of trophies. We take seats on the opposite wall, giving him some space.

"Vance, what is going on?" Jude asks him before I can zero in on the point that we're actually here about.

Our broody friend blows out a breath. "How could you tell?"

"You're acting like more of a scrooge than you normally do?" I suggest.

Jude hits me. "King, shut it."

I shrug, as I was just trying to tell the truth.

"Blimey, well … where to start?" He's quiet a second. "I don't know."

Now it's my turn. I rub his shoulder in what I hope is a comforting gesture. "Mate, we know you don't like to talk much. I talk enough for the three of us. But we're here, asking you to tell us what's bothering you. We can tell something isn't right. We're your family, and you're stuck with us."

He chuckles, low and sardonic-like. It's a bit eerie. "Funny you should mention family. Do you remember I told you about the girl I was seeing back home for a while? Lara?"

I remember him going home a lot, on weekends or off days, in the year *before* Jude and I left for RFC. But he stayed at the academy for a while, probably six months, while we were still there waiting to be called up to London. I thought it had just fizzled out.

"I didn't realize that was her name. Like we said, you don't really talk about ... well, anything." Jude cocks his head to the side, as if this has just dawned on him.

Vance nods, his long black hair almost down to his shoulders by now. "Yeah, I guess I should apologize about that. I just ... I don't like to talk. It feels ... excessive. We don't have to all unpack our feelings like a bunch of birds."

"But now, something is wrong?" I guess, knowing that if he's willing to talk, it must be bad.

He goes silent for a minute or two, looking down at his hands. And then, he looks straight at us. "Turns out, I got her pregnant. She had the baby and didn't tell me. Kept it. And now she's with some other bloke. Raising my baby."

The way he says it all, so matter of fact, nearly bowls me over. So many bombs dropped in one sentence that I can't even begin to compute. That's Vance though, holding it all in until everything piles up and spills over.

"Wha ... when ..." Jude seems to be in more shock than I am, because he can't even form a sentence.

"What did she have?" I ask, trying to start from the top of the question list running in my head.

Vance looks off, as if he's seeing something neither of us can. "A little boy. His name is Mason."

Mason. Vance has a son, and his name is Mason. "Blimey, you're a dad. A father. You have a son."

"One I've only met once, when I accidentally ran into her. The boy looks so much like me, I almost fainted on the spot." Vance chuckles, but it's a sad sound.

"She didn't even tell you about him?" Jude starts in, and I can tell he's in boss mode. He's going to call a lawyer after this, I can just tell.

"No, like I said, I didn't even know about the pregnancy. And now I wonder what I would have said if I had. Bloody hell, would I have wanted to be in his life given the chance? Would I have done something stupid, asked her to do something irreversible? And now she's with someone else. She's going to marry him."

Vance buries his head in his hands, and I can feel the agony in his words. He's in love with her. He wants to love his son.

"You love her." Jude realizes it a second after I do.

His head still in his hands, he nods. "I didn't mean to. She was just this girl from home, and it was a spur-of-the-moment thing. I'd fancied her for years, her parents live across the street from mine. It turned into more, and then one day she just stopped calling. She stopped answering my calls, and I thought it was for the best because I had to focus here and had other dreams. How could I let this happen?"

My heart breaks for my friend. He's in an impossible situation, and I can't even fathom having a child I wasn't aware of. Hell, if someone told me I'd fathered a baby, I'd be shaking in my boots. But all Vance wants to do is know his son. He's the best of us.

"What do you need us to do? What are you going to do?" Jude asks, gently laying a hand on his shoulder.

After a beat, Vance straightens up, his upper lip stiff. "I'm going to get them back."

33

KINGSTON

I'm back in London just about a month when shite hits the fan.

"Would you be able to come home with me for my sister's bridal shower?" Poppy asks.

I'm on my mobile, only sort of listening to her. "Uh ... I'm not sure. Might have a match, or practice. Actually, I think I have a product shoot with Jude's line next week, I should call his agent Barry to ask."

My musings are met with silence, which I don't realize until about five minutes later when I put down my mobile, and Poppy is staring at me like she's been doing so for a long time. Her mouth is pursed, and there is hell to pay in her eyes.

"So, you don't want to meet my family?"

Hold on, what? "I never said that—"

"No, it's fine. You're just too busy. Or maybe you just don't want me to take you home. That's not your scene, right?"

Um, has an alien invaded my girlfriend's body and turned her into a psycho bird? Or did I just miss a third of this conversation? Perhaps I'm going deaf because I have absolutely no idea what's going on.

"I knew it. All along, I knew not to get involved with you. That you didn't have the bollocks to commit to anything. That you wouldn't be man enough to actually be monogamous with me. Instead, I'm given some shite, flowery veil being pulled over my eyes. Did you really think that would work? That I wouldn't see right through your wishy-washy excuses?"

My brain is in panic mode, my heart beats wildly against my ribcage. "No, Poppy, listen, I'm not giving you excuses at all. It's just that there is a lot on my plate right now—"

"This is because I won't shag you, isn't it?" she demands, going from zero to a hundred in a second flat.

"What? Are you mad?"

"Oh, Kingston, just stop it. I'm as busy as you are, if not more. I travel more frequently, I keep later hours than you, my work schedule can change on a dime. The only difference is that I actually have some mature bones in my body. You can't seem to grasp that you're an adult now, that the decisions, or non-decisions, you make shape exactly the way you choose to live. Except this time, your hesitation doesn't just affect you. Put off being the champion football player we all know you can be, squander your talent, I don't care. That doesn't hurt anyone but you. But this? Your inability to be honest with me, to have an adult conversation about what we are to each other? It's pathetic and shows me exactly where I stand with you. Which apparently, is some muddled middle ground, just like everything else in your life."

Her opinion of me stings, and I wonder if she isn't so much talking out of anger as she really does think those things about me.

"That's not true and you know it. I've been with no one else. I've spent every spare moment with you. You know how I feel about you, how much I admire and respect you. If you really feel that way, I'm not sure why you're even with me."

Now I'm the one who's getting irrational.

"Is it because we haven't shagged yet? Is that what you need, to be inside me to commit to me fully? I apologize for being too slow on that front, perhaps it's too much to put up with dating a rape victim."

And in an instant, I'm irate. "Don't you even dare. I have *never* pressured you. I never even *think* about it. I haven't had sex in *months*, Poppy, and I have no feelings about it at all. I love being with you, however fast or slow you want to take things has never, ever crossed my mind. When you told me your truth, I took that burden on my own shoulders, too. Your pain is my pain. I'm fully committed. Where is this even coming from?"

And then, out of nowhere, Poppy bursts into tears.

I'm shaken to the core and rooted to the spot for a moment. For as much as she's dealt with in her life, Poppy has never seemed anything but tough as nails to me. Even when she told me about her rape, even when we had tender moments or those intense, silent conversations we've had with our eyes in bed.

"Come here, come here." I cradle her to my chest; loud, angry jolts of emotion shaking her entire body.

My heart breaks with each sound, and my mind is still on high alert because I have no idea what caused this outburst.

She clings to me, crying her pain into my T-shirt, for a few minutes while I rub her back. All I can do is try to comfort her, hold her, let her know from my embrace that I'm not going to let her fall.

After a few moments, when her breathing slows and her sobs turns into hiccups, she looks up at me with red-rimmed eyes.

"Going home ... it's got me all wonky. My family isn't the most supportive about my career, they're very religious you see. It's not exactly a welcoming committee when I show up. And especially not now. A while back, my dad cheated on my mum.

My upstanding, preaching father was having an affair with a local woman at our church, right under my mother's nose. I just ... after what happened with Nicolai, I have a very hard time trusting men. Or thinking highly of them in any way. Look how long it took me to let you in. And then I find out about my father doing that to my mother. It's just ... it's unbearable at times. The one man who is supposed to be holy and righteous, and even he can't resist being an arsehole. Sometimes I wish I could have a lobotomy, so that I didn't have to remember these things."

I smooth a few strands of her chocolate-colored hair, kissing the side of her temple. "I'm so sorry, love. I can't imagine the kind of hell you've been through. You should have no reason to trust men at all. And yet, it's part of the reason I admire you most. In New York, you told me you admire the qualities I look at as vulnerabilities in myself. I'm telling you the same. The fact that you're willing to trust me, to let me in, to cry on my shoulder after all you've gone through ... it is remarkable. I thank my lucky stars every day that you've given me chance after chance. That you allowed me in."

Poppy begins to cry again, and I have a feeling this has been a long time coming.

I hoist her up, carrying her as she sobs into my chest into her bedroom. I may be a daft male at times, but I know this breakdown is about much more than traveling back to her hometown or my involvement in her trip. I have a feeling that Poppy hasn't let anyone in her life close enough in a very long time. I've spent months with her now, and I guess I should have seen it earlier. She doesn't have friends, she doesn't call her mum to chat, she rarely goes out with girlfriends ...

She is alone.

Or, well, she has been.

In me, she has found someone she can count on and it must

terrify her. I know I'm scared half to death every time I think about how empty my life would be if I lost her.

For as long as she'll let me, I'm going to be her person. The one who protects her.

Her lion.

34

KINGSTON

"Where are we going? This is ridiculous, Kingston. You're going to ruin my makeup."

Poppy giggles as I make sure the blindfold is still secure, while we sit in the car carrying us through the darkness and energy of the London night.

"That's for me to know, and you to find out." I squeeze her thigh, loving the way her skin feels under my fingertips.

Bloody hell, my cock is struggling against the zipper of my pants in an attempt to fraternize with the beautiful goddess beside me. She's wearing some kind of short, sparkly dress that keeps riding up her thighs every time the car hits a bump in the road, and I want to scrap the whole idea of tonight and drag her to bed.

My intention *is* to take her to bed. I've proceeded with the utmost care and caution through the past couple of months. Phone sex, hitting each base one long period at a time, asking for permission each time I try something new. The only thing I haven't asked for is the consent to …

Make love to her?

That sounds like a cheesy way to put it, but I don't want to refer to it as shagging or fucking. When Poppy agrees to let me inside her, it's going to be so much more than that. Even now, when we're together, there is this ... feeling.

I can't quite describe it. You know those times in your life where the world just feels ... *more*? As if the universe is this minuscule thing and you're standing on top of it?

That's how being with Poppy makes me feel. Larger than life.

The driver stops the car in front of the restaurant, the twinkling light awning out front winking at me as I help Poppy from the vehicle.

"Kingston, can you please take this off?" she protests, folding her arms over her chest as I spin her to face the direction I want.

"Well, since you asked so nicely." Gently, careful not to ruin her perfectly made up face, I remove the blindfold.

Flourishing a hand, I wait for her vision to adjust. "Wait, you didn't—"

I'm too excited to let her finish the sentence. "Get us a reservation at Marin? Why, yes, I did. Our own personal boat ride on the Thames, complete with candlelight, five-star cuisine, and a world-renowned violinist. Happy four-month anniversary, love."

Puffing my chest out, I feel like Zeus presenting his queen with an entire planet as a gift. Poppy has been telling me for weeks how much she wanted to try this place. I've never done the attentive boyfriend thing, much less the boyfriend thing. I wanted to be, well, *great*. I want this night to be everything she's ever dreamed of when she's thought of romance, or of losing her virginity.

She inclines her head, grinning at me. "You remember the day we started dating? Also, I think you're supposed to let the romance speak for itself, instead of detailing it out like some vacation package you won on a TV game show. But it's so you, I'll forgive it."

"I want to give you everything you want." Wrapping my arms around her waist, I pull her in.

Poppy pushes up on the toes of those shag-me heels and gently lays a kiss on my lips. "Well done, Mr. Phillips."

When we check-in at the hostess stand, they let us know that they're preparing our Thames cruise, which is the crown jewel of the restaurant. It's been written about in the *Sunday Times* as one of the most breathtaking experiences of London you'll ever get so, of course, I wanted to give it to Poppy.

And in one swift second, everything I want this night to be goes up in smoke.

"That's him," Poppy sputters next to me, and I swing my gaze to check on my girlfriend.

Her hand is clutching at her throat as if all the air from her lungs just disappeared.

I turn, and instantly, I spot the man she's run away from twice in my presence. He's standing across the restaurant, leaning against the bar chatting up a girl who is definitely younger than me. As if I couldn't hate him more. Everything inside me seizes, and a ball of fiery anger, rage, and swift action lights me up from the chest out.

This is the man who hurt her. Raped her. Even thinking the word makes my blood boil. This adult male abused his power, took advantage of a naïve, innocent girl and stole the one thing no woman should ever have to give without consent. I want to murder him, strangle him with my bare hands until I see the light go out of his eyes.

But I'm not going to make a scene here. Sure, I want to rip that guy limb from limb. But that's not what Poppy needs. She needs someone who is going to stand by her side rather than go off like a powder keg, leaving her to balance on her own. She deserves the kind of protector who will care more about her well-being than showing off the power of his punch.

And besides that, I don't need my mug shot ending up in the papers. He's a famous photographer, one who carries way more clout in these circles than I do. Everything I've worked for since meeting Poppy, being demoted and fighting my way back ... I can't just throw that away.

It's best if I just get Poppy out of here.

"Come on, let's go home. We'll go back to Charlton House."

She's rooted to the spot, frozen as she stares at him. I'm almost tempted to snap a finger in front of her face, but she might tear it off. When I take hold of her hand, I find that she's trembling, and something in my gut rolls. I've never seen her like this, so exposed and raw. Not even in our most intimate or private of moments. One look at her face and I know she's terrified.

"Ah, look who we have here. Poppy Raymond."

The bastard eats up the short distance between where we stand and where Poppy just spotted him. Nicolai DeCallen, a name I've googled and a man I've murdered in my dreams, wreaks of evil. You can tell that, right down to his soul, he's rotten.

Neither Poppy nor I make any gesture of greeting. I think she's so terrified, she's lost her ability to speak. And me? I'm biting my tongue so hard I consume the metallic taste of blood. Perhaps if I don't say anything, the worst scenarios in my head will never play out.

"I see you've landed a new man, Poppy. A younger, flashier prototype." The wanker admires me, letting his sneer prickle over my skin. "Well, don't forget that I discovered you. You may have been a sweet little fawn, but I was the man who popped that sweet cherry, Bella."

A choked, gutted sound leaves her lips, and I see red. Here he is, in the middle of a room filled with throngs of people, openly mocking his rape victim. What in the world have we come to, as a society, as an industry, that this man feels comfortable airing his assault of a *girl* out in the open?

I get up, right in his face, my spit coating his nose as I clip out every word.

"What you did was rape a young girl. You abused her, lorded your power, and fundamentally changed her as a person forever. If I ever see you in her presence again, I will end you. I won't ask if you understand me, because I don't care. You are a swine, the most wretched human being I've ever met. And from this point forward, you will never see, speak to, or mention Poppy Raymond ever again. Or I mean it. I will obliterate you."

And with that, I grab Poppy's hand, forcing her feet to move as I drag her from Marin.

"You didn't … you didn't stand up for me. You barely said a word to him." The sassy, ravaging girl I know doubles over, seemingly defeated, as soon as we make it out into the night air.

Her voice is a hollow thing, and it's frightening me. "Poppy, it was better to just get out of there."

Her eyes are empty as she looks up at me. "The one man I thought I could count on, and you weren't there. I … I can't do this."

She straightens and turns, trying to bypass me. My arms shoots out, trying to hold on to some part of her, because I can feel our relationship quickly unraveling. I can't grasp the strings of our connection quick enough, and I can feel myself stumbling to catch up. But when I go to touch her, she recoils, and I know.

"Poppy, let me take you home. Right now is not the time. Don't do this."

How do I tell her that the only thing I was trying to do was protect her? That sometimes, a lion has to defend its pride by *not* engaging in a fight.

She's retreating, crawling back into the shell of self-protection I coaxed her out of.

"Don't follow me, Kingston."

I'm left standing on the street, my heart a shredded thing. If I look down, I wouldn't be surprised to see it bleeding out on the pavement.

35

POPPY

Two days later, a thirteen-year-old actress who posed for Nicolai on a movie set she was acting in, busts the world wide open when she begins criminal proceedings against him for rape.

When I first opened up the link that Claud texted me, reading the URL before reluctantly opening it, I thought the story was going to be some kind of convincing method my agent was using to get me to work with the bastard again.

And then the headline and picture loaded, and I dropped my phone on the hardwood floor. I couldn't bend to pick it up, it was as if every muscle in my body stopped working. I was paralyzed, and so many thoughts ran through my head.

In a way, I am free.

I no longer have to carry this enormous secret, this unspoken axe that split my heart in two every morning when I opened my eyes. It's a horrible thing to think that I'm not alone in my trauma, that there is someone else who was also hurt by Nicolai. Not being the only one is a mix of feeling relief that it wasn't just me who welcomed the assault, but also a huge amount of grief over not coming forward.

Over allowing this to happen to someone else because of my silence.

It turns out, he has dozens of victims. Girls in the entertainment industry, models, musicians, and even some of his staff. All of us were coming out of the woodwork, and each day, a new victim of Nicolai's, and her story, popped up in the news.

And as much as it ripped me apart from the inside out, made my stomach churn, turned my knees to pudding ... I could no longer stay silent.

The first person I called, after hearing the news, was Claud. He sent me the link, we'd danced around the truth of it for years, and I finally just came out and told him the story. My agent wept as I told him what happened to me and apologized profusely for never having given me the atmosphere to talk about it. In truth, that was partly my fault, and I told him as much. For a long time, I hadn't wanted to acknowledge that it even happened to me. But I did need to warn him about what would be coming, about how I'd need his help in the coming weeks, months and years.

Then, I rang Aria. I couldn't speak to Jude about this—not that he wouldn't find out. What I planned to do next, well, everyone would find out. But she was the one I trusted to keep it quiet, to help me arrange things, until I was ready to go public.

After I told her, she was silent for a very long time. I could hear the sniffling on the other end of the phone, and then she cleared her throat and said, "Tell me how I can help you take this bastard down."

That's how we got here, her holding my hand as we sit across from Jude's publicist, Barry McCathers, and the lawyer he hired to handle my case.

"You're sure you want to join the lawsuit. You'll have to testify. Your account will be public record, the media will get their hands on it," the lawyer, Anthony, tells me.

I nod. "He did this to so many other girls, who are so strong.

Especially the one who finally came forward, who faced her fear when so many of us could not. What kind of message would I be sending to her, someone so much younger than I am and so much braver, if I didn't stand up and share my story, too?"

Aria squeezes my hand and rubs the backside of it with her other hand. "You are stronger than anyone I've ever met."

With the smallest of smiles, I incline my head at her. "Only now, when I'm forced to be. But I'm trying."

We finish the meeting, going over every detail of filing my claim, as well as what will happen afterward. I know it's going to be chaos. Every media outlet in the world will be calling, trying to get every gritty detail of what he did to me. I'll have to wear the victim badge openly now which is something I never wanted.

But, like I said, I owe it to his other victims. I owe it to myself, if I'm being truly honest.

After the meeting, Aria takes me to our hidden cafe, the one I introduced her to. She pays for our cappuccinos, two pastries, and leads me to a table on the pavement.

I blow out a shaky breath, holding a hand to my stomach. "Why do I feel like I'm going to be sick?"

She smiles. "Because you're doing the right thing, even if it's scaring the living daylights out of you. It means you're a good person, the best of us."

"It doesn't feel that way."

"Give it time," Aria says.

We sit in silence for a few minutes, watching the odd person walk past the cafe.

"Kingston is worried sick." She breaks our contented quiet, and my stomach instantly knots.

As if she has to remind me of the biggest mistake I've ever made. It only took me about thirty minutes to realize I'd been a daft moron, lashing out at him for ... what? Not slitting Nicolai's throat right there and then? Blimey, I'm a twit. I wanted someone to blame, for someone to feel the pure agony I'd been feeling at that moment.

He was the closest thing, the easiest one to hurt just as much as I'd been hurting. And I was wrong. So bloody wrong.

What Kingston did for me, holding his composure, not reverting to his old ways but making sure I was his first priority to protect ... it was everything I'd asked him to become over the last few months. He had been a *man*, the kind that was fiercely loyal and focused on my well-being, rather than a pissing contest with someone who wasn't worthy in the least bit of either of our anger or time.

Of course, I saw that now. But how could I go back to him like this? I am an injured fawn, some creature caught in the crosshairs of chaos. I don't know how long it will take to get back to the strong, independent woman he'd taken to.

"He doesn't need to worry. I'll be fine." The waitress sets down our steaming mugs, and I take a sip to busy my hands.

"Poppy, you don't need to play that game with me. I'm the queen of covering up my emotions. And I also tried to convince myself that none of it mattered. It nearly killed me and almost wrecked everything Jude and I have. Don't make the same mistake."

I sigh. "Aria, Kingston and I are not you and Jude. We're dysfunctional and broken, and my life is about to become loads more complicated. He's fragile, his newfound confidence hangs in the balance. He has so much he needs to focus on, least of all a woman with the kind of issues I'm dealing with."

Aria tsks her tongue. "Old me would have agreed with you because she thought it protected the man she fell in love with. New me wants to smack you in the face. Kingston is one of the most devoted, loving, attentive people I know, once he's given the chance to be. As for your complications, I'd say that's his choice to make if he wants to be a part of them or not, not yours. Let him make it. Don't shut out the love being offered up to you on a silver platter. It's the best gift you'll ever be offered. And if you turn it down, you're even more of a daft model than I thought you were."

She winks, signaling that the last part of her campaign speech for Kingston is just the kick in the trousers she thinks I need.

The only thing I keep hearing though is that what Kingston is offering me is ... *love*.

36

KINGSTON

"Nice defending, Phillips!"

One of the Rogue coach's calls out from the sideline, the mesh jersey over my practice kit moving in the wind as I punt the ball across the field.

Being back on the RFC pitch, in the stadium, a part of the team ... it's done with a whole new set of eyes. I've been part of the organization since I was seven, but I never truly took it seriously until my first practice back about two weeks ago.

It's as if I just discovered soccer, this energy source that lights up my veins and makes living easier. With every cut of my boots in the grass, every kick of the ball, every play I learn and every piece of knowledge I remember about the sport I love I fall back into this codependent relationship with it. Our first match, an off-season friendly that many of the starters will sit out, is in another two weeks. Niles told me I'll be on the pitch from the opening whistle, and from that moment on, the competitive energy to let loose in a game has been pumping through me.

I also have nothing else to focus on to keep me from sinking into the doldrums of my heart-wrenching breakup, so I've been funneling everything I have into my play.

When Poppy walked away from me, it was the most difficult thing I've ever had to endure. I fought every instinct that told me to storm after her, to take what I want. In the past, I would have. I wouldn't have taken no for an answer, I would have done more damage by forcing her to confront me, or her vulnerabilities.

More than my own past, or the family I grew up in, more than being sent to Narta or finding out what Nicolai had done to Poppy.

Losing her crushed me more than anything in my life ever had.

And knowing that I had to stand by and just feel it, rather than do something about, has been the toughest realization I've ever made. But, I had to do it.

I won't be attempting to be the man she wants me to be if I don't. Poppy needs space and time to heal, to grapple with the reality of her world now that everyone knows about what happened when she was fifteen. Every time I see a news report or receive an alert on my phone, a thunderbolt of sadness splits my heart even wider. The woman I've fallen in love with is hurting, and I have to be strong enough to respect her wish of not wanting me around.

Fallen in love with ... how is that for irony? The first and only woman I'll ever love, doesn't want me to be in love with her.

It guts me that I can't be there for her. That she's shut me out, that I can't knock down her door with my fist and demand she let me comfort her.

The worst part is that she's right there, within an arm's length.

Shaking my head to clear the fog of dejection, I pass to Jude, who sprints the ball up the field as if it's easier than sitting down on the couch. He flicks it with his boot, skirting one of our teammates on the other side of the pitch, and sends it soaring into the goal past Remus.

We all cheer, though not too gloatingly because we are playing our squad. Remus shoots a pistol finger at Jude, swearing about how that'll be the only one he ever sinks in the back of the net on his watch.

I move back to my position, grinding my boots into the grass, waiting for the next drill we're going to run.

"Feels good, eh, mate?" Jude jogs up alongside of me, sweat dripping from his face.

"Like the good old days, except I care more and am not thinking about the girl I'm going to shag tonight." I grin, trying to keep the despair from my expression.

I'm positive my best friend sees it anyway.

"Have you seen Poppy?" he asks gently.

Well, I guess he can see right through to my wonky mood. "No, I'm trying to give her space."

"That's a first. Bugger, I'd be impressed if I wasn't so against you respecting her wishes."

A whistle sounds, signaling a break to grab water or a quick bite. I don't feel much like either, so instead, I plop down on the grass, collapsing to my back and looking up through the giant opening in the roof of the stadium.

"What do you mean? You've been on my back for years to be an upstanding citizen, and now I'm trying to be, and you want me to be dodgy again?"

Jude sits down next to me, leaning back on his elbows to glance up at the clouds. "You're Kingston Phillips, you can't be fully upstanding. We all expect a little recklessness and obnoxious behavior from you. Case in point, I think you should knock down Poppy's door and tell her you love her."

Has he been reading my thoughts? The idea is so similar to the one I've been having, and so preposterous, that a hiccup of laughter explodes from my throat.

"Who says I love her?"

"That pathetic puppy dog pout you've been wearing since she ran out on you at Marin says it." Jude shrugs.

"Harsh, mate."

"But true. Take it from one lovesick man to another; you're bloody toast. Well-done, burnt to a crisp, in love. I knew it from the minute Poppy walked into that club and told you off ... you've been in love with her for a long time. Maybe before you realized it. And you wouldn't be Kingston if you didn't shove that fact down her throat."

"Don't you talk about her throat," I half-joke, trying to make light of the heavy conversation he's trying to have.

"See, that right there! Pure Phillips teasing. Now take some of that scoundrel spirit and go after her, mate. She needs you, even if she thinks what she needs is space. Loving her, smothering her with it, is the best thing you can give her right now."

The organ in my chest both beats double-time and cowers in fear.

I give voice to the one thing that's been cycling through my mind since Poppy told me not to follow her. It's the big bad wolf of fears, that one that's lived inside my head since before she came into my life.

The fear that I care for someone, and all they will see me as is a nuisance. Just like my own parents.

"What if ... what if she doesn't want my love?"

Jude raises an eyebrow, looking down at me. "Pshh, mate, you're Kingston Bloody Phillips, she'd be daft not to want your love. Besides, Aria all but told me Poppy does."

Ah, yes, now I remember why I keep him around. The inside access.

I guess it's time to pull one last prank, though I won't be joking and there will be no fool if all goes to plan.

There will only be us, Poppy and I, solidly together.

37

POPPY

After I file my case, joining the thirty-three other women Nicolai DeCallen raped or assaulted over the years, my world implodes.

The media coverage of Poppy Raymond coming out with her story has been ... catastrophic. My face is splashed on every newspaper, telly, social media site, and every possible form of communication in between. I had to have Claud shut down the number to my mobile and get me a new one. I deactivated my Facebook and Instagram accounts. I can't turn on the television or listen to the radio.

Not because I think that telling my truth was a mistake because I adamantly agree it wasn't. I'm glad it's out, that I don't have this dirty little secret corroding my soul any longer.

But having to hear people's opinions on it, the talking head commentators or the Internet trolls ... I want no part of it. They don't know what he did to me; they don't know how I feel. It's incredible what people believe is their business to discuss and pass judgment on.

The front desk called up ten minutes ago, saying something had arrived in the post for me and could they bring it up. I didn't really want them to, but the staff at Charlton House are so polite and kind; they've been steadfast in protecting my privacy the past few weeks. So, I agreed.

Opening my door when the bell chimes, wary that the doorman is about to ask me questions I don't ever want to answer, I'm stunned at who is waiting on the other side.

"Just give me a minute." He holds up his hands as if I might bolt.

Blimey, he looks dishy. I've always been a lost cause when he grows that stubble out, all the golden facial hair making him look like some sort of caveman. And if it's possible, being back at RFC has toned his arms even more than they already were. For a split second, I fantasize about all of those muscles working in tandem as he hovers over me on a bed—

"I can't stay away any longer." Those jade green eyes bore right into me.

Of course, I've thought about him being just on the other side of my wall. I've heard him bumbling around in there, have pressed my ear to the paint to listen. Has he moved on? Maybe he's seeing someone else.

Surely, his insistent phone calls and text messages would say otherwise, but I wouldn't truly know. I haven't answered any of them.

How can two people, who live right next door to one and other, seem oceans apart?

Because I made it that way. Made it impossible to get close to me again.

Apparently, Kingston isn't listening any longer.

"Kingston, I—" I'm about to tell him that I've been an idiot, that I'm a fool for ever shutting him out.

That I'm in love with him, and the only thing I want more than Nicolai in prison for what he's done, is to be in Kingston's arms as the trial starts and the world falls down around me. Because if he's there with me, I can be brave.

He holds up a hand. "I didn't sock the guy's lights out because I'm trying to be more. *For you.* I don't want to be the bloke who just reacts without thinking about the consequences. Because the consequence of pummeling that bloody wanker into the floorboards would be that I don't get to stand by you. That I don't get to hold your hand through the roughest time of your life, because I know this is going to be really bloody hard, Poppy. I want you to be able to lean on me, and you wouldn't be able to do that if I got myself thrown out of the club and sent to play football in Siberia or something. I decided not to engage in immature, daft behavior so that I could stand by you as the man you deserve. And if you're mad about that, then you're mental. I mean, I know you're mental, but even more than I already thought. Can't you see, I bloody love you. I would only try to play the smart move for you; I'll only ever be in love with you. So, just fucking let me."

His diatribe shocks me so profoundly to the core that I think I stand there with my mouth wide open for more than two minutes. I just stare at him, this beautiful, brilliant, broken man who is healing himself so that he can heal me.

"I ... I'm in love with you, too. So I must be mental. Blimey, who falls in love with their arse of a neighbor that they can't stand?"

Kingston swoops me up into his arms, spinning us until I'm dizzy and can no longer feel the sting of our interaction with Nicolai or the dread about the trial to come.

"You did, you gorgeous woman. And I'm damn thrilled you did, since I'd probably be passed out in some pub in Nova Scotia, playing D-league football. Poppy, I didn't realize all I had to live for until I met you. That sounds bloody cheesy, but it's true. You smacked some sense into me, made me realize that I could take control of the way I was living. And you can do the same thing, love."

We're quiet as I twine my arms behind his neck and hug him to me. The feeling is exquisite, chasing the loneliness and despair out of my heart in an instant. I was a fool to believe I didn't need this man.

"You couldn't at least have slugged him? Just once?" I tilt my head to the side, smirking at him.

"Do you want me in a jail cell, or holding your hand in the courtroom at his trial?" Kingston twists a lock of my hair through his fingers.

Sighing, I let my forehead drop to his chest. "I don't know if I can do it. Go through my account of things again, face him ... face the media. Everyone will know, Kingston."

"And I will be right here. What can I do? What will help? A cup of tea?"

An idea blossoms, not in my head, but in my heart. I say the words before I can second guess them.

"Take me to bed. Be the first man to make love to me. Be the only man to show me what it feels like when two people love each other."

And without hesitation, Kingston lets me lead him into my flat.

38

POPPY

My hand isn't shaking, but calm and steady as Kingston's eyes sweep over me.

Standing before my bed, fingertips intertwined, I feel nothing at this moment but pure, raw *love*.

Part of me always wondered how I would feel when I finally decided to lose my virginity. Most of it had been taken from me without permission, an abuse of my body and my sexual decisions just stolen. But when I finally got to decide, would it be with doubts?

Would there be fear about lying down with a man and letting him enter me in the most intimate way possible? Would I be able to go through with it, knowing how much pain and trauma I'd been through?

But as Kingston brings his hands up to my face and delivers one of the deepest kisses I'll ever experience, the sensation rolling all the way down to my toes; I have no uncertainty.

My mind is a haze of lust, pleasure, love, and affection; the only thing I want to do is watch Kingston enchant my body while I do the same to him.

His fingers inch my leggings down, and I want to scream at

him to both hurry up and take his time. I'm burning up as I watch the top of Kingston's sandy blond mop as it descends down my body. When he gets to my nipples, still encased in my camisole tank, his wet, hot saliva hits the material over each nipple. I groan, the sensation almost too much for me to take.

"You taste amazing, even like this." His words make the place between my thighs burn.

Together, we lie down, moving over the plane of the mattress together. Our hands undress, the dance of sex which we've been practicing but haven't completed thus far. We've become exceptional at this, creating our own numbers and steps to follow. I pull his shirt over his head; he slips the straps of my shirt or bra down. My bottoms have usually been disposed of earlier, and I trace the lines in his back and shoulders, sucking on the sensitive spot of his earlobe, as he pulls off my top and underwear.

Kingston's rough hands run down my body, skimming over the lines of it and teasing at the sensitive spots. His fingers creep lower, as do mine, both of us yearning to touch the other and hear the noises we make together.

He finds my center first, dipping a finger tentatively inside and using the wetness that coats it to rub at the sensitive bud between my thighs. As he mesmerizes my body, using all of those magical skills he possesses, I unbuckle his jeans and push them past his hips. His boxers snag on them, giving way as I push, and his erection springs free.

My lord, the man is big in every aspect of his figure. I've been introduced before, having tasted and gripped the beautiful piece of anatomy. There is something powerful in being able to shut a man like Kingston Phillips up. And when he came ...

Just thinking about it now makes me flush and more wetness pools low in my core.

Kingston adds a finger to where he's working my opening,

pressing a knuckle past my lips until I groan from the erotic stretching.

"I love you," he whispers as he fingers me, his mouth coming down on mine.

The sensations become overwhelming, swamping my system as the tension he's building with his touch pulls tighter and tighter, until ...

My legs go rigid, a careening wail exploding from my throat as I climax and the edges of my vision go white. Kingston holds me, his lips still on mine and his fingers still inside me until I'm panting and spent.

"Kingston. I'm ready," I whisper, everything inside of me tingling from the orgasm.

My muscles are relaxed, and every part of me is sure that this is the right moment.

He sits up, and I hear the clink of his belt on the floor as he shuffles through his jeans. Kingston comes back up with a condom, rolling it onto his pulsing erection. I watch as the latex sheaths over him and wonder for a brief moment if this will hurt.

Of course, I've had his fingers inside of me. After the first time I gave him permission to enter me that way, and it only hurt for a few seconds. Each time after, the pleasure built deeper and deeper, until Kingston was giving me climaxes I hadn't even thought were possible.

I lie back, spreading my legs for him. I'm so wet and hot that just that motion makes me hurdle toward the edge of another orgasm. Kingston moves over me, nudging my thighs open. Just the size of his broad torso, much less the endowment hanging between his legs, should be intimidating but it isn't. Because I'm focused on his expression; one of pure love, aimed right at me.

"Look at me." He grunts, and I can tell he's losing control but trying to grasp at the reins. "This is going to be uncomfortable, but I think it will be better if I just do it quickly. Grab me, bite me, do whatever you need to do to dull the pain. This is about *you*. And if, for any reason, you want to stop, you tell me."

Kingston's eyes, his heartfelt plea and command, beg me to understand. Beg me to tell him yes.

I nod; my entire body throbbing with the need to be one with him.

And, as if I've unleashed the beast, he thrusts into me in one, smooth motion.

I keep my eyes locked on his as I let out a breathy, pained cry, adjusting to the invasion. The searing burn of his knob deep inside me has me inching away, but even the movement brings a stab of pain. I cling to Kingston, fighting back tears as my nails dig into his shoulder blades.

Just as I'm about to tell him it's too much, the pain begins to dull. The uncomfortable sensation abates, giving way to something ... delicious. The tingles unfurl from my core outward, and I wiggle, not to get away but to further explore it.

"You. Okay?" A strained groan comes from his lips.

I bring his gaze to mine, using my hands to capture the sides of his face. "I love you. You're not hurting me. Make love to me."

"Poppy ..." He pulls almost all the way out and pumps into me again, making me whimper.

"Kingston ..." His name is a breath I expel as he picks up, the go-ahead I've given an invitation to lose himself.

And this is the dance I've been waiting my whole life to experience, with the one partner I'd always wished to find.

"I love you, I love you, love you ..." It's a chant he's repeating, a madman brought to the brink. By me.

Kingston slams into me, holding himself there while he comes. I watch the euphoria light up his face, the way he tenses but completely relaxes all at once.

"Oh, yes. We're definitely going to need to do that again." I giggle, my voice hoarse, as I stroke my fingers up and down his back.

"And again, and again." He nods against my temple. "As soon as I can catch my breath."

He'd stolen mine, and I wasn't sure I ever wanted it back.

39

KINGSTON

"Kiss your man, he scored a goal."

I rub my cheek into hers as she tries to push me away, chuckling as my fresh-out-of-the-shower hair drizzles droplets onto her shirt.

"Ugh, you're wet. Kingston, stop!" Poppy swats at me, but it's no use.

I scored a goal in my first match back, and the first one Poppy's ever sat in the family suite for, so I deserve some snogging.

"You know you'll have to come to every game now and sit in the exact spot, right?" I tell her.

She eyes me. "I didn't realize you were so superstitious. You do know that's all a load of codswallop, right?"

Shaking my head, I dip my head for another kiss. "Nope. You have to be here from now on, every match."

Huffing, she takes my hand and leads me out of the room. "I have my own career, and a burgeoning position at the Females Against Abuse nonprofit."

I love it when she gets all independent and cheeky with me.

"Love, I'm kidding. Our season will suffer, but you'll have the career you want."

Poppy makes a face as if she might throttle me, or impale me with the dagger of her high heel. Since the night I stormed her door and she gave me her virginity, we're back to our old dynamic. Pissing each other off, sarcastic barbs, steamy snogging, couple things.

Only now, we get to shag. And I get to explore all of her.

Every. Single. Part.

I thought I was on top of the world before, but I'd been a bloody wanker.

It's taken a long time, and many hard lessons, to get to where I am. But now that I'm here, I fight every day to keep what I desire most.

Two days ago, we attended her sister's bridal shower. Poppy finally brought me home to meet her family, and while they were somewhat put off by my boisterous, London personality I think they took to me. Her sister, Tabitha, seemed the most smitten with the fact that I really love Poppy. The two women may not have many similarities anymore, but it's good to know that she wants to see her little sister happy.

They'd even all sat down as a family and discussed what had happened to Poppy, and what was about to come out about it. Her mother wept, and her sister reached out to hold her hand. Her father looked stricken and said if she needed them to come up for the trial, they would. It was a touching moment, though I have a feeling Poppy will spare them from most of the details in the coming year.

Nicolai DeCallen's trial date has been set, for five months from now. Every single one of the cases against him have been granted into the Crown Prosecution Service, meaning they have no statute of limitations. In all, there are forty-seven women accusing him of rape and sexual abuse. But none more famous than Poppy, who is being both torn apart and held up on a pedestal in the media. Not that we listen to any of it. For the past two weeks, we've gone about our obligations, her campaigns, and my playing. Aside from that, Poppy has started a nonprofit, with some of the other victims, that helps survivors of rape or domestic abuse receive therapy, housing when needed, medical treatment, and so on. The work she's doing, it's so bloody admirable. That this woman can get up every morning and help people experiencing the same trauma that sometimes still gives her nightmares—it's more than most people will ever do with their lives.

And when we're not at work, we rotate between each other's flats, cooking dinner together or reading books. Mostly, we spend hours in bed, making up for the time we didn't make love.

And love it is. The way I feel about Poppy is all-consuming, this humongous ball of emotion that sometimes I can't even give words to. It's not just that either, that draws me to her.

I think the reason we were meant to find each other, why we match so well, is that we never found anyone who so perfectly fits us like I do her or she does me. All our lives, we've been cast aside or told we don't belong.

It was only because we were waiting for each other.

She is my perfect fit.

Jude and Aria asked to double date after our match, but before it even started Poppy texted that she wanted to head to Charlton House after. She's not up for hitting the town much, these days, and I respect that. This too shall pass, but if she needs to batten down the hatches, then I'll bloody batten them.

As the lift brings us to our penthouse floor, I hold her in my arms, her head lying on my chest. How far we've come since that first drunken ride.

"So, where are we staying tonight?" I ask, swinging our

conjoined hands as we come to stand in the middle of our two doors.

Poppy grins. "My bed is more comfortable."

"Yes, but my flat has better snacks," I counter.

"Or maybe, we should spend the last night of summer in our favorite spot." Poppy's smile is devilish.

"The pool," we say at the same time as we race for the lift.

Poor Mrs. Clemens, her penthouse floor was about to get a lot naughtier. Perhaps I need to do something about our separate living situations.

As the ding of the doors signals our race to the pool, I let Poppy get a little farther ahead, watching as she strips down to her bare, beautiful skin and launches herself into the water.

I thought I'd been half in love with the gorgeous model who'd given me a tongue-lashing in the club those months ago. But I had no idea just how spectacular she really is.

And like the woman I love once said, I'm her lion. I'm going to protect that shine of hers at all costs.

Even if it means jumping bare arsed into a pool to save her from drowning with my very-skilled mouth.

EPILOGUE
POPPY

Six Months Later

Kingston drops a box on the restored hardwood floors, and something rattles dangerously inside.

"Watch it, would you?" I glare, but my voice carries no scolding.

Immediately, he eats up the space between us, and hoists me into the air. "What you going to do about it, love? Because if you want to spank me, I'm all for it."

My hands grip his shoulders as I roll my eyes. "Oh, I'm sure that would be a real consequence for you, babe."

Slowly, he lets me slide down his body until we're pressed together and his hands flirt above the waist of my jeans. "I'd take it like a man."

"Yeah well, this woman has about fifteen more boxes to unpack in the kitchen, so why don't you make yourself useful and tell the moving blokes where to set up the bedroom furniture?"

Kingston's eyebrows waggle at me, and he plants a quick kiss on my mouth. "I can certainly do that. You know, setting up the bedroom furniture is the first part of my plan to start christening this entire house—"

I slap a hand over his lips. "There are people everywhere, you naughty man."

He lands a gentle smack on my arse and then lopes off with a smirk on his face. The cheeky, dishy scoundrel.

Turning back to the white and blush kitchen I've helped design over the last month, a huge smile perks my face up. Today, we're moving into *our* brownstone in Belgravia. After spending a month arguing over whose flat we should stay at on any given night, Kingston had thrown his hands up and suggested we just buy a home together. At first, I told him he was mental. But it had only taken six hours in my bed for him to convince me of just how wonderful living in our own multi-level townhome would be.

And I have to admit, he was right. We bought a three-story townhome on a quiet side street in our favorite neighborhood the week after he convinced me and started work on it right away. A new kitchen, new hardwoods on the second floor, and a claw-foot tub in the master bathroom. We put in an office in one of the spare bedrooms, complete with frames of some of my most iconic campaigns, and a few of Kingston's framed kits.

Of course, he'd given me design control, but I hadn't made our home *too* feminine. It was just enough that I was happy, and so was he.

Out of the corner of my eye, I see the movers bring in the giant wood-paneled game table Kingston had in his Charlton House flat. What grown man wants a Foosball table in the middle of the dining room? The man I love, that's who. I'd outlawed it from the start, but the thing was getting prime real estate in Kingston's man cave in the basement.

I watch as the man of the house directs traffic, and catches me staring. He saunters away with his hips swinging, and I wonder to myself, not for the first time, how I am so lucky to end up with that jokester?

Although we live in London, approximately ten minutes away from them, we haven't seen Kingston's parents since he ordered his father to leave Charlton House. As much as I think my boyfriend is still bitter and traumatized by their behavior, it's better for him and his mental health that there is no contact.

My family, on the other hand, has been surprisingly supportive. They all came up for the first day of the trial last month, even though I told them it wasn't necessary. Tabitha held my hand in the courtroom, and although they won't be here when my testimony is heard in a couple of days, I have the support system I need.

Kingston will be with me every step of the way, and Aria and Jude already assured me they'll be in the room. Aria told me that if I ever feel myself clamming up, or about to break down, all I need to do is look at her. Tell my story to her.

Since my story came out, when I was named on the list of victims, life has been ... unsettled. Although falling in love and starting our life together has happened at the same time this media circus is progressing, providing a nice distraction, it's always there in the background. The day I'll have to get on the stand looms over our heads, and I'm ready for it to be over with. Soon enough, we'll know Nicolai's fate. I hope he's sentenced to years rotting away in a cell.

Today is a happy day, though, I try to readjust my mood as I bend down to begin unpacking the next box.

"Why do you have a box labeled 'Not for Poppy's Eyes'? What, is there a bunch of kit chaser's knickers in here or something?" I joke, opening the box anyway as he smirks at me.

"More like stacks of old *Playboy* mags. I didn't think you'd want to know about them before I stash them under the mattress." The teasing tone of his voice is light and comes from somewhere behind me.

Only, when I open the cardboard box, there is one small, velvet box sitting in the middle of it. Instantly, my heart begins to hammer in my chest.

"What is this?" I'm scared to even reach for it, and my eyes go wide when they flick up to meet his.

"Pick it up," Kingston breathes.

The small jewelry box is a crushed blue velvet and fits in the palm of my hand. Gingerly, I bring it to my chest, too nervous and stunned to do much else.

"Turn around, Poppy."

When I do, Kingston is on one knee before me. The tears come instantly, and I have to blink them out to clear my vision as they fall down my cheeks.

"I love you. We're making a life together, but I don't just want to be roommates, or in a relationship. It seems too insignificant for what you mean to me. So, I want you to be my wife. Please, give me the honor?"

When I first met Kingston, I wanted nothing to do with him. But he changed me. He charmed me. He showed me the true colors inside his soul, while also revealing mine.

I've given so many of my firsts to this man. And now I'm going to give him one more.

"Yes. *Blimey*, yes." I'm too shocked to say much else.

Kingston is beaming as he slides a princess-cut diamond onto my ring finger and then stands to envelop me. I squeeze him tight, wanting to drink this moment in and never let it go.

"I ... I can't believe you just proposed." I giggle, pulling back to stare at him.

"I can't believe I made you speechless." He gives me a haughty grin.

Pressing my lips to his temple, then cheek, then the tip of his nose, I admonish him. "Don't count on that happening again."

"Want to bet?" Kingston's hands slide down to my waist.

"Oh, you're on, Phillips."

It's going to be a lifetime of challenging each other, and I can hardly wait.

Thank you for reading! Ready to find out who Vance falls for? Read his second chance, surprise baby romance, <u>The Mighty Anchor!</u>

Read the rest of The Rogue Academy series, available now!

The Second Coming
The Lion Heart
The Mighty Anchor

ALSO BY CARRIE AARONS

Do you want your **FREE** Carrie Aarons eBook?

All you have to do is **sign up for my newsletter**, and you'll immediately receive your free book!

Then, check out all of my books, available in Kindle Unlimited!

Standalones:

If Only in My Dreams

Foes & Cons

Love at First Fight

Nerdy Little Secret

That's the Way I Loved You

Fool Me Twice

Hometown Heartless

The Tenth Girl

You're the One I Don't Want

Privileged

Elite

Red Card

Down We'll Come, Baby

As Long As You Hate Me

On Thin Ice

All the Frogs in Manhattan

Save the Date

Melt

When Stars Burn Out

Ghost in His Eyes

Kissed by Reality

The Prospect Street Series:

Then You Saw Me

The Callahan Family Series:

Warning Track

Stealing Home

Check Swing

Control Artist

Tagging Up

The Rogue Academy Series:

The Second Coming

The Lion Heart

The Mighty Anchor

The Nash Brothers Series:

Fleeting

Forgiven

Flutter

Falter

The Flipped Series:

Blind Landing

Grasping Air

The Captive Heart Duet:

Lost

Found

The Over the Fence Series:

Pitching to Win

Hitting to Win

Catching to Win

Box Sets:

The Nash Brothers Box Set

The Complete Captive Heart Duet

The Over the Fence Box Set

ABOUT THE AUTHOR

Author of romance novels such as Fool Me Twice and Love at First Fight, Carrie Aarons writes books that are just as swoon-worthy as they are sarcastic. A former journalist, she prefers the love stories of her imagination, and the athleisure dress code, much better.

When she isn't writing, Carrie is busy binging reality TV, having a love/hate relationship with cardio, and trying not to burn dinner. She lives in the suburbs of New Jersey with her husband, two children and ninety-pound rescue pup.

Please join her readers group, Carrie's Charmers, to get the latest on new books, exclusive excerpts and fun giveaways.

You can also find Carrie at these places:
Website
Amazon
Facebook
Instagram
TikTok
Goodreads

Made in the USA
Middletown, DE
29 October 2021

51290813R00158